PENGUIN BOOKS

INHERITANCE

Livi Michael has three previously published novels, *Under a Thin Moon*, which won the Arthur Welton Prize; *Their Angel Reach*, which won the Geoffrey Faber Memorial Prize and a Society of Authors Award; and *All the Dark Air*, which also received an award from the Society of Authors. *Inheritance* is her first novel on the Penguin list.

INHERITANCE

Livi Michael

PENGUIN BOOKS

PENGUIN BOOKS

Published by the Penguin Group
Penguin Books Ltd, 27 Wrights Lane, London W8 5TZ, England
Penguin Putnam Inc., 375 Hudson Street, New York, New York 10014, USA
Penguin Books Australia Ltd, Ringwood, Victoria, Australia
Penguin Books Canada Ltd, 10 Alcorn Avenue, Toronto, Ontario, Canada M4V 3B2
Penguin Books India (P) Ltd, 11 Community Centre, Panchsheel Park,
New Delhi – 110 017, India
Penguin Books (NZ) Ltd, Cnr Rosedale and Airborne Roads,
Albany, Auckland, New Zealand
Penguin Books (South Africa) (Pty) Ltd, 5 Watkins Street, Denver Ext 4,
Johannesburg 2094, South Africa

Penguin Books Ltd, Registered Offices: Harmondsworth, Middlesex, England

First published by Viking 2000
Published in Penguin Books 2001
1

Copyright © Livi Michael, 2000
All rights reserved

The moral right of the author has been asserted

The landscape and history of Saddleworth have been two of the inspirations behind this
novel. Many of the people who live there are far more informed than I am, and will be
aware that this is an imaginative rather than an historically accurate rendition of the area.
Any resemblance to actual persons, living or dead is purely, coincidental

Inheritance developed from two previously published short stories: 'Robinson Crusoe', which
appears in *The City Life Book of Manchester Short Stories* (Penguin, 1999), and 'Blue Sky Like
Water', which appears in *Shorts: New Writing for Granta* (Granta Books, 1998)

Copyright still applies to the work of Ammon Wrigley

Set in Monotype Sabon
Printed in England by Clays Ltd, St Ives plc

To my mother, Ann (1927–99), who was unlike the mother in this book.

Rare to smile
She sometimes sang.

This enduring landscape
Smiles in sunlight
Sometimes sings.

from 'Yorkshire Mother', Hilda Cotterill (1912–99)

Acknowledgements

I feel that this book has been almost a collective enterprise from the start. My thanks are especially due to Ian, for practical support and help with the family trees; to the librarians of Uppermill and especially Judith Lamb, for the loan of a room in which to write; to Saddleworth Museum for facilitating my research; to Terry Eckersley whose thesis *The History of Saddleworth Workhouse* (1986) was particularly useful; to Norah Brown and Kate Swann for long conversations about the history of Saddleworth and its workhouse; to Chris Alt, Penny Hinke and Wendy Raphael for reading the manuscript in its most distressed state, and offering good advice; to my agent Clare and editors Juliet and Hannah, for a similar service later on. Perhaps most of all I feel that thanks are due to the poet and historian Ammon Wrigley, whose life's work preserved the distinctive flavour of his locality and language.

A separate, large thank you to the Society of Authors, whose generosity bought me some time in which to write.

CHAPTER I

Louise

The day my mother died I sat by the hospital bed, watching the sun rise. The world flooded with colour as it drained from my mother. Nurses wheeled trolleys along the corridor outside as they always did, an old man shuffled to the toilet, and a flock of pigeons rose up against the window in a slow, flapping curve.

I was in that stage of exhaustion where I simply sat and stared, as a child in a pram will, at all things equally. There were stripy shadows in the blond fields, and far away a bus went by, flashing and winking. My mind ran on, throwing out thoughts and the shapes of thoughts, like paint on a spinning disc throws colour.

I remembered those rare occasions when I took her shopping, the way she lingered over the fruit and veg, the deep green of broccoli, the dusty purple of plums, with her mouth slightly parted and moist. She would cup oranges and scarlet peppers in the palms of her hands, rarely buying, just testing. Her hesitation had little to do with price, or eventual use. I remember her touching fruit like paw-paw, which she never knew the name of and would never use, in a delicate, questioning way. Once I saw her surreptitiously sniff one, then quickly put it back.

I don't know when this love affair with colour and with the feel of things began. In my childhood, everything in the house was beige. Only in her old age, in Morrison's, could she indulge this unexpected, lavish side.

I remember following her, the quality of her attention attracting me, that aura of seriousness and care that seemed to expand around her. I hovered in the penumbra of it, entranced and hungry. It was a kind of tenderness that she was never able to give, so far as I remember, in any other circumstances at all.

Later, in her emptied front room, I sat on a fold-up chair, listening to the profound silence she must have listened to as her deafness increased in this quiet house. I had sorted about a thousand boxes of stuff, old bills, old letters, old tights, ornaments, accounts. Did my mother do accounts? Her shopping, birthdays, bills, any extra items of expenditure, were all carefully written down, added up, deducted from her pension, then left on scraps of paper stuffed in drawers. All that reckoning up, I think, and then you die.

As her only child I have inherited the contents of all these drawers, bills and receipts going back twenty years, postcards from people she hardly knew. Behind my mother's neat, judgemental façade lay all this chaos stuffed in drawers. There was even a bread bin in the meter cupboard, stuffed full of woolly hats. I packed up her clothes – even the oldest of them, full of holes, weren't thrown away – and made about twenty trips to Age Concern. A van came for the larger items of furniture. The council wanted the keys back as soon as possible, but there was a lot of stuff left that I couldn't bring myself to take a decision about. I packed everything I could into my car, then left the remaining boxes with her neighbour, Mrs Harris, promising to return soon. Then I sat on the folding chair, in the empty room, with its lighter squares and grey marks on the beige walls where the pictures used to be, the stains on the carpet obvious now the furniture was gone.

Is this it? I thought. Is this all?

I felt her presence powerfully, not only in the room but in my body, my flesh and bones. Though I never resembled her, I could feel the shape of my body occupying the same space as hers, and when I got up, finally, it was with the awkward stiffness of the elderly. I closed the door behind me, left the keys at the local office, drove away.

Only much later, after a second death, do I find the album.

CHAPTER 2

It is an old album with a leather cover. It has been carefully preserved, unlike most of her photos, which were in miscellaneous packets and envelopes stuffed in cupboards. It is right at the bottom of one of the boxes I brought back, that I had almost decided to throw away. I sit down in my London flat, just off the Euston Road, and open this album from another time and place.

I've seen most of these photos before: my mother and her sister as little girls, holding banner ribbons at the Whit Walks, on donkeys on Blackpool beach, their mother, Lilian, holding one baby then two.

Here are some of my father's family. Not many, my mother never did like them. But sometime during her eighteen years of widowhood she must have relented and put a few in this small album: my father as a little boy with his mother, his grandfather. There are four of the wedding – Susan Millicent Armitage (fastidious, correct) giving her hand in marriage to Ernest Peter Kenworthy (unworthy but likeable) – then three of the baptism of their only child, me, Louise Anne Kenworthy. Only surviving child I should say, for here is a photo of my little brother, Peter, who died in his cot when he was four months old. There's another of me holding him. I am less than three years old. I look anxious, but determined. I didn't know there were any photos of my little brother. She kept them hidden all these years.

Here's another one she must have slipped in sometime before she died – Great-uncle Albert with his tremendous beard. I've seen

3

the same photo in some cousin's house but I never knew we had one. Great-uncle Albert was prone to bankruptcy and embezzlement. That might have been forgiven if two other families hadn't emerged when he was sent down – a former wife and a current mistress, each with children. We still have the newspaper cuttings. I'm surprised Great-uncle Albert ever made it into my mother's album; perhaps thoughts of death mellowed her. Or perhaps she just got tired.

This is not the oldest photo. There are some here I've never seen before, including one of Albert's parents, my great-grandparents. Anne and Edward on their wedding day, it says on the back in thin, spidery handwriting.

Then there is this one. Anne again on her wedding day, looking magisterial in an enormous hat. On one side of her there is a woman and on the other a girl, perhaps thirteen or fourteen years old. Both hold small bouquets to Anne's large one; none of them is smiling. The woman is shorter and darker than Anne, slightly dumpy; the girl is quite tall, but anxious-looking and very frail.

I take the photo out and examine the back. No information there. But I have seen it before.

I am nine or ten years old, in my parents' bedroom. My mother is looking through a drawer for some paper or other, and a clutter of postcards and envelopes falls out, this photo among them.

– Who's this, Mam? I say. – What's she called?

My mother mutters something in a preoccupied way.

– What? I say. – What, Mam?

– That's your great-grandmother, she says, without looking round. – Get your feet off that bed.

– But who are they, Mam? I say. – The other ones.

She glances back briefly. – I think they're her sisters.

– What are they called?

– I don't know.

– How old are they?

– I don't know. Don't put your mucky fingers all over it.

– Was she the oldest? I say, pressing Anne's face.

– Stop mauling that picture about, my mother says, taking it off me.

– Was she?

– No. I don't think so.

I remember being surprised, since she was the biggest.

My mother held the picture for a moment, looking at it closely. I craned round her shoulder. A thought occurred to me. – Do I look like her? I said, pointing this time to the girl.

– Haven't I got enough to do without answering twenty questions?

My mother picked up all the papers at once and packed them into the drawer. When I asked again I was told to give over mithering. Then the next time I looked, sneakily, when my mother wasn't there, I couldn't find it, and when, some time later, I asked her about it, she pretended not to remember.

She was good at that.

Now, over thirty years later, the same question occurs to me. Do I look like the girl in the photo?

The question used to be important to me, an only child who resembled neither parent. My best friend Linda looked like her brother, Neil. Next door but one the McTavishes, seven of them, all looked like one another. Front teeth fell out, scars came and went, two of them wore glasses, otherwise it would have been hard to tell them apart. My mother looked like her mother but not her sister. As she got older, however, she looked more and more like her grandmother, Anne: short and dumpy rather than magisterial, but very fair and with the same pronounced chin. My father had jet black hair and was handsome, I thought. I didn't look like him. I was fairish but slight, and without my mother's jawline. A quiet, mousy, observing child.

– A changeling that one, I heard someone say once. Or, to our faces, She's a little elf, your Louise.

If Peter had lived maybe he would have looked like me. We would have been Louise and Peter Kenworthy, going to school together, then to Cubs and Brownies, football and dancing. We would have fought, of course. Maybe he would have looked like my dad.

5

I bet my dad wondered about that too.

I can't say they ever made me feel as though they were wondering. I didn't ever feel, as it is sometimes said people do, that they would have preferred him to live rather than me; never felt anything other than special to my poor, feckless father.

Here is another memory. I am three, maybe four years old, sitting on the doorstep in a square of light. The sky is very blue, as it always is in my childhood memories, as if only when I was thirteen did it start to rain. There is no one to play with. I haven't met Linda yet and the McTavishes are far too rough, my mother says. But I do have, as the only child is sometimes said to have, an imaginary friend.

My mother moves around the kitchen, passing back and forth, then suddenly comes over and stands behind me, puts her towel down, listens.

– Who are you talking to? she says, then as I carry on, Louise, who are you talking to?

– No one, I say, not liking the interruption. – Just a friend.

– What friend?

I don't want to look at her, I know she'll tell me there's no one there.

– What's your friend's name?

I turn round finally to look at her, but she is in shade. – Peter, I say.

My mother picks her towel up, then puts it down again, then walks out of the room.

I don't claim clairvoyance. I must have heard the name mentioned. When I wasn't playing I was watching and listening.

– She misses nothing, that one, my grandmother said regularly.

Or maybe it was memory, one of the little tricks memory plays. The haunting game.

Whatever it was, my mother never asked me again. And I learned not to play with Peter when she was there. Gradually I stopped playing with him altogether. And the problem of who I looked like stopped troubling me. I grew up, tried different clothes and hairstyles, took a fashion course, became a buyer. I moved away from home, visited less and less. Even my voice changed. Now here I am, ten months after the death of my mother, looking at that same photograph. I was right, all those years ago, I think, looking at the face of that young, serious girl. She looks as if she might have been taller than me, but the bones are the same and the fine, mousy hair (I dye it). Her eyes are light. I can't tell the colour, but they might, like mine, be grey-green. It wouldn't be very obvious now, I think, putting the photo back. Here I am, forty-three years old, with my dyed hair and makeup, but the resemblance is definitely there. It is an inheritance of sorts, I suppose. The only one I'm ever likely to have. A pity, I think, that since most of my relatives seem either to be dead or overseas, I'm unlikely to find out any more about her.

Even so, as I pack my case for the journey I have to make, I think twice then slip the album in.

Hours later, I sit tucked into a corner of the little train from Manchester. The afternoon is heavy and overcast with sudden flares of light. Through the window I catch glimpses of the CIS building, Strangeways, a scrapyard and a huge estate. Great cranes swing and dip at the start of the new motorway, there are stripy shadows in a yellow field. Close by, all these things flicker into one another, like a video on fast forward; further away they are still.

As we approach the hills of Broadstones the temperature dips and the colours darken. The little train rattles into a tunnel and in my head I'm saying, This is a mistake, this is a mistake, in time to the drumming of the engine and the wheels.

But I had to come back. I told Edie Harris a few weeks and it's been almost a year.

I don't drive any more, I can't imagine ever driving again, yet I'm returning to a place where public transport was bad before deregulation, and since has practically disappeared. And, of course, there is no taxi at the station, so I haul my bags past Rejects Direct, Carpet Warehouse (1000s of roll ends), second-hand shops with cookers and chairs on the pavement.

Then the houses: rows of dirt-grained terraces with no gardens, where people grow flowers out of sinks and buckets, chimney-pots and the cracks in stone walls. Only the new houses have gardens, or rather, squares of lawn with no partition between them, great staring windows.

Where have all the bus stops gone? There are only roadworks with cones and signs. My arms will be trailing along the ground before I find a bus, and I can no longer remember the way.

Finally I find someone to ask, a man with a beard and a check shirt. He has the face of a folk singer, he will stick his finger in his ear and sing when I ask.

– Two, three miles that way, he says, and I stare at him aghast. I thought it was nearer, but then the last time I came I was in the car.

– Is there a bus? I say, and he jerks out his thumb, indicating the road that leaves the village for the moor.

I totter along it with my huge bags, conscious of my smart shoes scraping the ground.

I pass council houses like the ones I used to live in. I can hear old children singing, *I-rye-chicorye, chicorye, chicorye, rooney pooney, om-pom-piney, alabaster, whiskers, Chinese chink.*

There is a row of terraces, then another row, then a shop, closed, then more roadworks. Then, a long way past the roadworks, I see a bus stop. And there are two people standing by it, which seems hopeful to me, and I stagger and lunge towards it and drop all my bags around it with an ecstatic sigh.

The two other people, an elderly man and woman, barely glance my way. They gaze out over the moor with a fathomless patience, and the farsightedness of those for whom waiting and not knowing is a condition of existence. If I looked into their eyes I would see the changing landscape reflected: farms and mills and factories coming and going, railways, cars and churches, people, trees.

Gradually I orientate myself. It is a great brown landscape, unending as a lament. Immediately before me there is a stony hillside, with sheep dotted among the stones, motionless as if planted. This is surely Blackshaw Edge. On the other side of it there is the workhouse, a great stone building where the poor were driven and never came out. And when my father had been drinking or betting my mother would cry and moan and say we would all end up there, and only much, much later did I realize that it had long since closed down.

Time falls away like peel.

I feel as though I'm existing in different centuries simultaneously. The jagged rocks before me stipple the hillside like the gravestones of a thousand handloom weavers; to my left, wooden staves have been driven into the ground to test the land for new buildings.

Time passes.

I sigh suggestively and look at my watch.

No one moves.

I clear my throat and hook the old man's eye.

– Is the bus due? I say. My voice, the voice I have acquired in London, sounds ridiculous here.

The old man smiles helplessly at the old woman, who says, There's not been any buses down here for a while.

– But – this is a bus stop? I suggest, in London tones.

– Not any more, the old man says.

– Not for a long time, says the old woman.

– A long long time, says the old man.

I stare at them, start to say something then stop and pick up my bags. I step away smartly, conscious of my smartness, my footsteps tapping and clicking on the road.

Jesus Christ, I'm thinking. No wonder I left.

– Ere, ere, the old man calls out suddenly. – It's ere.

When I turn round they are both waving their arms at me in excitement. There is a bus. It looks as if it's been cobbled together from the remains of other buses, but it is still a bus. The driver doesn't have a timetable: when I ask him how often the buses run he says he just does what he's told. I sit down, thankful for a seat.

What I'm looking for now is the track to Hurst's cottages, since one of them, as he told me on the phone, is empty.

– It's damp, he told me. – No heating, not much furniture.

– I'm sure I'll manage.

– Gutters leak, he said. – Drains are blocked.

– That's fine.

– No one's been in it for years, he said. – It smells. And the windows won't open.

– You've sold it to me, I say.

Pause.

– Wife'll do it up for you.

– Oh, no, she doesn't have to.

– You'll need bedding.

– I won't have a car.

Pause. No questions, no surprise.

– Wife'll sort out bedding.

Packing, I hesitate over my radio and mobile phone, then decide to be firm.

Then, after all, pack both.

The road curves widely round the hill. More terraces appear, more roadworks. Then, finally, a path, leading off the road and twisting round. The bus driver obligingly lets me off, though there is no sign of a stop, and I pick up my bags again. At the end of the path two cottages lean together as if propping one another up. The one on the right is empty.

Here I am, Louise Kenworthy, standing in front of Henry Hurst's one vacant cottage.

– Key's under stone, he said, like a wizard speaking runic. But sure enough by the brown door there is a stone and beneath it a key. I fiddle with the slightly rusty lock until it opens.

Inside the front door there are wood shavings, leaves and paper bags. Woodlice scurry away from my feet. There is a sheet of paper with green print on it: The Blackshaw and Harrop Residents Association invite you to, it says, then it's torn. I crumple it in my hand. There is junk mail, of course, and a local paper. Henry must call in from time to time, because there is only one paper. I step carefully out of the hallway into a bare, brown room, which as I enter is full of light, then suddenly drab and cool. There is a battered settee and a table, both pushed against one wall. The next room is the kitchen. It has three cupboards containing pots and a yellowing cooker. Upstairs there is a bedroom with no curtains. Bedding is at the foot of an enormous bed, and there is a cupboard for my clothes. The smaller room has been made into a bathroom. The toilet works. I rub my aching shoulders then go back downstairs and pull my bags inside. I unpack a few things, including my mother's album that I have brought with me in case anyone can tell me anything about the photographs. Then I go outside, to stave off a sense of impending doom.

I won't be here long, I tell myself. Just long enough to pick up the remaining things of my mother's, and maybe ask a few questions about my family tree.

There are no other reasons I want to think about.

It has an unusual garden, this cottage, at the top of a stone wall, to one side of the house and round the back. Behind it is the moor, stippled with millstone grit and sheep. Stare at it long enough and it is hard to believe in London. The memories I have of it come and go like so many droppings.

Here I am, Louise Kenworthy, standing in the garden of Henry Hurst's cottage, which I have been mad enough to rent.

The path is overgrown with tall feathery grass and cow parsley. An enormous elder tree hangs over the garden to the wall of the house, as if pushing it over. Dead blossoms straggle from a laburnum tree and beneath it there is a fallen branch. When I sit on this, tiny reddish beetles scurry in formation along the crevices of bark.

I have the sense of the slow opening out of time.

– Ragged Robin, my father says, pointing to a tall plant with pink petals. – What is it?

– Ragged Robin, I say.

I must have been about three at the time, walking along a wall, holding his hand.

It must have been about the time that Peter died.

The bushes that divide my garden from my neighbours' rustle, and a face appears among the foliage like a withered peony.

– Staying here long? it says.

– I don't know, I reply.

– We'll be neighbours, then, the face says. – Mary. Mary Butterworth.

I make my way over to the gap in the roses.

– Louise, I say. – Louise Kenworthy.

– Not Susan's girl?

So much for anonymity.

– I used to go to school with your mother.

The first person I speak to used to go to school with my mother.

– She was a lot younger than me, though.

I say the expected thing.

– Oh, yes, she was. I'm seventy-six, you know. She was one of the littl'uns when I was leaving. But there was only one school then. I was sorry to hear about her, though, very sorry.

She shakes her head and sighs.

– Would you like a cup of tea?

I'm desperate for a cup of tea. I follow her through the gap in the roses down the stone steps from the garden to her kitchen, which is smaller, darker and smellier than mine.

Mary looks like Charles Laughton in a pinny and sagging tights, straggly grey hair poked behind each purplish ear. From her I learn that tenants in the cottage I'm in have come and gone, but it's been empty for nearly two years (they don't last), that there's a problem with the drains and Henry Hurst is always saying he'll sort it out (but never does), that Mary herself has been here nearly forty years (I've seen them come and go). When I ask her about shopping she tells me that there is a bus, twice a day, that stops near the Co-op in Greenbridge (but not that near), that the little shop I passed on the way up is open every day except today (but sells nowt), that I can get Henry Hurst to deliver eggs and milk and yoghurt. Mary's son brings her veg from his allotment, most people drive to the large Asda seven miles away.

When she asks me why I'm here I'm vague. I say, as if rehearsing it, that there are one or two things to sort out after my mother's death. She seems to accept this; as a rehearsal it goes OK. And she obviously has me sussed as a city-dwelling incompetent, because when I leave she presses tea, milk, butter and home-made bread on me, dismissing my gratitude with a Go on, get out.

The angle of light is changing. I had forgotten how, in the evenings, the light becomes sombre and pure. I make myself tea and toast, read the local paper. There is a residents' battle over the mill and its pond, someone's baby has just won a prize. As I read these things a powerful feeling of strangeness descends. I walk from one window to another, staring out, but the lights are on so I can only see a reflection of the room I'm in. I rub my fingers against the rough plaster of the walls. This is a habit I have had since childhood, testing things by touch. I can't bring myself to turn the lights off, as if I sense another, palpable presence.

Later, I lie in bed reading, as moths flit and butt into the bulb (no lightshade), trying not to notice the blank black square of window (no curtains) or the tapping of the elder against the pane. When I turn off the light, finally, the window makes a pale square on the opposite wall. In it a daddy-long-legs climbs restlessly, ceaselessly, falling down and starting again, convinced that the square of light is the window. I have been afraid of the dark, very afraid, but I hoped things would be different here. I won't put the lights back on but leave my radio running. I turn my face trying to find a cool place on the pillow, resist the idea of picking up the phone.

In the morning I am wakened by the hum of many bees.

There are no bees.

For several moments I lie in that limbo between sleep and waking. There is a feeling of expansion towards a surface, or skin of consciousness I can't quite break through. The buzzing noise increases and with it a sensation of despair. I will be sucked back into the dream I have only half left, the one in which he is waiting for me in the empty room. In sleep my body remembers everything about him, his touch and taste. My eyes shift uneasily beneath lids that won't open, my breathing is so shallow it barely disturbs my ribs. Finally I wrench myself awake, but the light is so bright, impossibly bright as though my pupils have been winched open, that I cannot keep my eyes open. I reach down and fumble for the radio, turn it off, realize that the noise is coming from outside.

It's happening again, the action replay of everything I thought I had left behind. Behind closed eyes I suffer the terrible sensation of fall. I put a foot out but do not trust the floor, as though its surface tension might, pulled by a different gravity, disintegrate and I would find myself slipping into the space between, the universe of space between atoms.

Is this what it is to be a ghost?

Carefully, carefully across the floor, pressing the door I make my way over to the window on the landing, where the noise is very loud, and try unsuccessfully to open it. Nothing insubstantial here. It is, as Henry Hurst said, stuck, the frame rotten. I'm afraid to press it too hard. Craning my neck I make out roadworks and a sign – NYNEX.

And it's only eight fifteen.

I'm relieved that the night is over, but the feeling of strangeness doesn't go. I walk round the house, looking out of all the windows, seeing, as if from a great distance, the uneven distribution of settlement up the hillsides. The hills are like the backs of camels, bearing uneven loads.

I focus on the road below, which is called Shaw Road. It winds on for ever, flanked by the great brown hills. Along it at intervals blackened terraces stand in blocks of six or eight: Weaver's Row, Factory View, Mill Cottages. I used to play with a girl from Mill Cottages before I met Linda. Traffic along the road is sporadic. I watch as a woman crosses reading the *Radio Times*. She doesn't look up even once.

This is not the Euston Road.

It has rained in the night and the earth is soaked. When I open the back door I can smell the garden. At the front door there is a note for me from Henry about the milk and a bottle of milk with tiny slugs clinging to it. This is the real world, I remind myself. There are things to do. I wash and dress, make more tea and toast, draw up a list. I have to go to the house of my mother's neighbour, pick up and sort out the things I left there after the funeral.

I have to shop.

Finally, overcoming a massive reluctance, I slip on a jacket and set off down the track to the road, glancing over the moor as I go.

I had forgotten all this, huge clouds and the shadows of clouds shifting across the hills. I had forgotten how strong and sweet dog-rose smells after heavy rain, when the blossoms stop being crumpled, how snails gather in the crevices of stone walls or cling to the stems of cow parsley.

Everything else has changed. There are boarded-up shops and factories, new housing estates encroaching further and further up the hills. There is no sign of farm workers, only a solitary tractor spraying a field with something that smoulders on the earth. The old engineering works that occasionally employed my father makes plastics now. I get nearer to the area where I used to live, pausing only to buy a packet of cigarettes, for although I have given up smoking I can tell I will need a fag for this.

These are all the areas of my childhood, where I skipped rope, played hopscotch or ball, often alone, usually alone, then later walked arm in arm with Linda in our scarlet platform shoes. Round every corner I expect to see ghosts of myself playing hide and seek with the woman I am now, looking for lost places or waiting with a melancholy, observant eye.

Then I come to the street where I used to live.

The sensation of having died, gone to heaven and been kicked out again is even stronger here – kids I don't know playing in the road, men I don't know under cars. And all the time, in the background, are the waiting hills, where dingy sheep munch indifferently on.

Edie has been expecting me.

– Eee, love, I do miss your mam.

– How are you doing?

There is a cup of tea and a cake and memories of my mother, sitting in the garden, talking over the fence, working for charity.

– She'd always time for you, Susan.

– You knew you could always call.

– She were always one for a joke.

This is a mother I never knew.

I avoid looking out of the window at the garden where I used to play, wonder if Edie still keeps lollies in her fridge for the children next door.

The boxes, two of them, sit on the settee. One is smaller than the other.

– You're in a car, of course, says Edie.

– Well – no.

– *No?* . . . Eee, love . . . however will you manage?

– I'll be fine.

– We can always drop them off for you.

About the only thing I understand clearly is that I don't want visitors, but Edie won't be fended off. Her Trevor will deliver the boxes later – he knows the cottages. I'm obliged to be grateful but decline lunch. I have to shop sometime.

– *My* mother died twenty-two years ago, she says, as I leave. – And I still think about her. She's still here. She punches her chest, and there are tears in her eyes, as if time has never passed, I think, as if somewhere inside us we never acknowledge the passing of time. But I'm not up to dealing with Edie Harris's grief. I make my excuses quickly and leave.

I eat lunch at a pub I used to know. It's called the Boat and used to be a smoky little dive where old men played pool. Now, of course, it's all laminated surfaces, mirrors and naval trappings. It overlooks the canal, near where the proposed marina will be built. I eat Starboard Salad, with croûtons in the shape of tiny anchors. But I can't stay here long, ignoring covert glances. I have to find the shops.

In the end I find three shops, though this takes up most of

the afternoon. I buy toilet rolls, marmalade, washing-up liquid, sausages, potatoes. I had thought of making chilli, but bangers and mash will have to do. On the way out I study the adverts in the window: babysitter required, Gameboy with games, bike for sale.

Bike. Now there's a thought, I think, trudging once again up the hill. It's a gentle incline and the bag isn't heavy, but by the time I get back I'm bathed in sweat. And everything I do is effortful. I wash and change again, wonder where the nearest launderette is. It occurs to me that I could make wine from the elderflowers in the garden. If I had cider vinegar. Or sugar. If I was going to stay here that long.

I make toast and marmalade and stand in my new doorway smoking the cigarettes I shouldn't have bought, watching out for Trevor and the boxes.

Unlike his mother, Trevor is uncommunicative. He parks his car on the main road and between us we carry the boxes up the path. He declines a cup of tea and leaves without asking questions, which suits me fine. Later I stand at my door with another cigarette, watching the evening sky go pale, then deep. I feel oppressed suddenly, as though the sky has flattened itself against the earth. I am remembering what it was like to be a child again, pressed up against the banisters on the bedroom landing, listening to my mother's voice hectoring my father. On and on it went, he had no right being married, no right to have a child. Her voice rises in volume and pitch. She wants the response he won't give. I am crying with my mouth open, begging God to make her stop. But all that's over now, and I'm very cold. I go back inside.

All that's left of my mother is in these boxes. I always knew there would be nothing to inherit but detritus, the things she always meant to throw away. Even so, in the absence of an inheritance, these odds and ends have assumed an oppressive importance. It's as though I have inherited a negative: an image of what the boxes are not, memories of what my mother was not. And all the time the things I always meant to do with her – invite her to stay in my flat, show her round London – stand in my memory like art objects in abandoned rooms.

It is hard to make myself open the boxes. I run my finger along the harsh edge of each cardboard flap, then methodically fold it back. There is nothing remarkable. A few books (doctor and nurse romances), more bills and receipts, an exercise book of mine from school containing stories I wrote at eight – about a fairy princess, a party and a storm (star, tick, very good). There is a house and a snowman in a plastic ball, and when I turn it over, snow falls. There are shoe trees and a china dog. Then there is a prayer book, leatherbound, scuffed edges. I open this looking for evidence of our family tree: dates, names. But the only writing inside is in a thin, smudged copperplate: *20 March 1904*, it says. It is not the same writing that is on the back of the photographs in my mother's album.

I turn it over in my hands.

The past is the past, I think.

I can feel the past all around me, like dust.

I handle each object carefully, turning it round, examining it before putting it back neatly, so they all fit in the one box. As I do this I feel tremble inside me the kind of tenderness for her I have been warding off all my life. It is an awkward, trembling tenderness. I don't want to stop touching these objects that were hers. I run my fingers over them, I close my eyes. It is as though I will learn more about her by touching them, as though I was a blind woman in a garden, waiting for rain to map out a landscape for me, by falling on leaves, or water.

Finally everything is put away, except the prayer book, which I put next to the album on the table. Two mysteries from my mother's life.

Most mysteries should be left alone, I think.

Suddenly I'm restless. Though it's evening I want to go out. I slip my jacket on again, telling myself that if I pass an off-licence I might buy some whisky to help me sleep: you need alcohol in a place like this.

But I avoid the shops, make my way to the canal. Not the kind of thing I would do in London, but here, on this warm evening, there are plenty of people about and more lamps than I remember. The more I walk the more memories come back to me. I remember being in Manchester with my mother. She is walking ahead of me in a brisk, bent-forwards kind of way, because she hates the city so much. I like it, so many people, so much to see.

– Come on, Louise, she keeps saying. – Get a move on.

We pass a long building with huge blank windows, one after the other, dark so that all I can see in them is the reflection of me. Here I am with my leg outstretched, here flinging my arm out, here mid-jump. A procession of different Louises.

Massed leaves darken the water, but there are lights from new houses along the banks and an old mill that has been turned into flats. What happens to memories when all the places you used to be have gone? Orange lights make bright patterns in the black water. The reflection of a lamp is not the same shape as the lamp but a thin, wavering line. Not the thing itself, but a transmutation of that thing. That is like memory, I think.

CHAPTER 3

From somewhere I have dredged up the recipe for elderflower wine. Seven heads of elderflower steeped in water, with sugar, lemon and cider vinegar. The bush is passing out of flower, but there are seven heads left. And I have water, but none of the other ingredients.

Although I know this is a sad waste of time, I go to the shop. It is a grocer's, but in the window there are tie-neck blouses with large dots, tartan skirts and wellies. Inside, mop and bucket sets are propped up against the sugar, garden forks and rakes next to tinned peas.

Two shop assistants stand by the till. One has a square face and a challenging haircut, the other, pale, delicate features and long black hair tied back. She is half hidden behind the magazine rack, and appears to be dabbing her eyes.

– It just doesn't seem right, she's saying.

I pick up a bag of sugar, no lemons, and smile. – Matches, please, I say.

Square-face plants the matches down on the counter without a word.

– Do you have any lemons?

– Lemons, Cath, she bellows suddenly, without taking her eyes off me.

– We've got bottled, Cath quavers, from behind the counter.

Square-face jerks her head at me. – Over there, she says, and obediently I wander off, past tinned carrots, sweetcorn, jars of pickle.

LIVI MICHAEL

I can hear Cath saying, . . . leaving her there like that –
– More fool her, says Square-face, the hard.
I hesitate over the bottled lemon juice – really the recipe requires peel. And there is no sign of cider vinegar. Cautiously I approach the counter again. Square-face is looking at Cath as if she might be about to eat her, Cath looks sorrowfully down.
– You know what she's like, says Square-face.
– Yes, I do, says Cath, but I still feel sorry for her.
I smile in a hovering kind of way.
– It was evil, what she did, says Square-face.
– Oh, Joan –
– Evil.
They become conscious of me at the same time.
– Cider vinegar? I say, without hope.
– Cider vinegar, Cath, bellows Joan.
– We've got malt vinegar, Cath offers.
I shake my head, prepare to leave.
– We've got apples, Joan says, in a challenging way. She's right, of course. I could *make* the cider vinegar before making the elderflower wine.
I leave the shop with two pounds of apples and a bottle of Sarson's.
Buckets, I think. I'll need buckets. Or big pans.
When I get back I am brisk and efficient, clearing out cupboards and sweeping the floor. This is me, Louise Kenworthy, keeping house.
Not a bucket in sight and none of the pans is big enough.
Thwarted, I wander into the garden, where thistles are beginning to tangle with the nettles, making any pathway completely inaccessible.
It is a summer of dull, humid days and sudden, bouncing rains. After rain the greens are very pure with a blue light in them, there is a fresh, living smell.
I've forgotten about having a garden, what to do. Every day there is something different to see. Poppies unfolding from large furry

22

pods, tiny beetles crawling over stone. When I part the leaves of a fern I see two bright winged creatures mating; their tiny, trembling movements.

Other tenants have made forays into the garden. There is a clump of marguerites near the wall, and a small hydrangea. But I don't want to make my presence felt.

I could go back to London tomorrow, I tell myself. The only reason I'm still here is indecision. I could go back and face it all again, face what going back might mean.

Mary's voice floats despondently over the hedge.

– Drilling again. There's always someone digging up that road. I wish they'd find what they were looking for. They can't dig owt up without drilling through some bugger else's pipes. Who asked for Nynex anyhow?

I have already noticed that whenever I go into the garden, Mary goes into hers. Sooner or later her voice, which sounds like Eeyore's might sound, drifts over. She is apparently talking to herself, so I never know whether or not to reply. Now, however, I make my way over to the hedge. – You don't know, I say suddenly, how I could get to the supermarket from here.

Pause. I have cut her soliloquy in two like a worm.

– Why? she says.

– Well – I could do with some cider vinegar – and the shop doesn't have any –

– *Them*, Mary says, they never have owt. I've got some in if you want some.

– Really?

I step closer to the roses and the smell is strong and sweet.

– I always keep some in. Good for gallstones. Clears the blood. But them two in shop know nowt. What do you want it for?

I remember this well. The way my mother would offer something so aggressively it felt like an attack. Take it the wrong way if you want to, see if I care.

– Elderflower wine, I say meekly, and Mary's grim face almost relaxes.

– My mother used to make that. You've got to be careful how you bottle it up.

Bottles, I think. I haven't got as far as bottles.

– Half a cupful do you? Mary says.

– You don't have a large pan, do you? I call after her retreating back.

She soon returns with both vinegar and pan, and a long list of instructions. I don't mind. It's weirdly comforting. Like standing in front of my mother. This is also the first conversation I've had all day, apart from the shop. I'd forgotten how silence can gather inside your head, and how, at the end of a day without speaking, you have to clear your throat just to see if it will work.

– And don't fill the bottles right up, she reminds me finally, or corks'll be coming through walls.

I thank her and promise her a bottle when it's ready, and go back down the steps to the house, snapping off heads of elderflower as I go.

Steep them in a pan full of water with vinegar, sugar, a drop of lemon and a few chunks of apple instead of the peel. And I do have bottles, plastic ones full of water, which I empty into cups and pans. I hum in a distracted way. This is me, Louise Kenworthy, making wine like Delia Smith. Or like that Edwardian lady whose country diary I've never read.

The great thing about elderflower wine is that it only takes a couple of weeks and is dead simple. I can give all the bottles to Mary if I decide to leave.

The bad thing is that once it's all got together in a pan there's nothing else to do.

And it's not even lunchtime yet.

I stare out at the garden.

Everything in nature is busy except me.

It's a kind of torture, not being busy.

I don't know how to do this. I think I will go mad.

I go back into the lounge, feeling colour burn unexpectedly in my face. There is the album, next to the prayer book. I open it at the picture of Anne and her sisters, trace round the youngest sister's face with the tip of my finger.

Her lips and cheeks have been tinted by the photographer, her hat is dark. She is printed there, for ever, at the beginning of this century, me at the end of it, two world wars between. Nothing bridges that gap, I tell myself. Then I think about the stray gene that has printed the ghost of her into my features, my body. I think of it appearing and disappearing in the family line past and future, winking its way through eternity.

I don't even know her name.

I do have family round here: my mother's cousins, their children. Most of the children will have moved (no jobs), but it shouldn't be too hard to find out if any of them are still around. One of them, surely, might know something about this girl.

CHAPTER 4

Martha

One night, in the first month of their marriage, Martha's husband said to her, Martha, there is something I must tell you. I'm afraid, Martha – sometimes I'm afraid – that my soul – is possessed by the Devil.

Martha laid down her spoon. Pike off, tha gawmless boggart, was what she thought. – I wish you would not say such things, Charles, she said.

Charles said nothing for some time. He remained looking downwards, pressing the middle finger of each hand to his temples. After a long moment he said, No – no – you are right.

Martha picked up her spoon again, and after another moment, Charles picked up his.

CHAPTER 5

Louise

It's a fine Saturday morning and I'm climbing a hill, towards a handsome, well-appointed, eighteenth-century house, stone-built, panoramic views, three garages.

I can hear the estate agent's patter in my head, but I can hardly imagine the kind of money you'd need to buy this place. It does belong to someone in my family, though. I've drawn out the relationship this way.

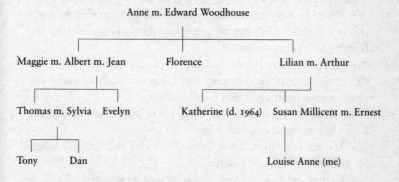

I'm going to see Dan Woodhouse, barrister and second cousin. He doesn't know this yet. If I'd phoned he might have put me off, so I'm relying on the element of surprise. I have some qualms about doing this, but I'm here now and the gate is open so I walk past the Range Rover in the drive and ring the bell before I change my mind.

Frenzied barking.

I turn and look at the view, which extends all the way to Manchester.

Frenzied barking followed by muffled cursing.

It's half past ten on a summery morning, small clouds chasing bigger ones over the hills. But obviously not everyone is up yet.

When the door opens several wolves fly out. A man I assume to be my second cousin is on the other end of them, holding many leashes. I step back as he attempts to haul the hounds into a side room.

– Sorry, he mutters, finally slamming the door on them.

– Nice dogs, I say, with my early-morning smile.

– What?

He looks definitely last nightish, blurred and stubbly, unwashed. Unamused.

– I'm sorry to call on you like this, I say, in a more propitiatory way. – It's Dan, isn't it? Dan Woodhouse? You don't know me but we are related. And I'm doing some research into my family tree.

– What? he says again. Not awake yet. I'm beginning to think this is a mistake. I fish out the paper on which I have scribbled the family tree and pass it to him.

– You must think I'm crazy, I say. – I should have written. Only I'm in the area at the moment, and I was out walking and – my mother once mentioned that you lived here . . .

I trail off and watch him reading. He is stout and balding. He looks like no one I can remember.

– My mother Susan, I say, helpfully. – Her mother was Lilian Woodhouse, before she married.

Glimmerings of something, some kind of recognition.

– I'll come another time, I say.

At the same time he says, You'd better come in.

I follow him in, over muddy, trodden newspaper, past the renewed frenzy of the dogs, to an enormous room with beams and a giant fireplace. Dan takes out cigarettes and waves at the settee. – Sit down. If you can find a space.

He has a point, for though the settee is one of those long, curving ones sometimes seen on American TV, every inch of it is littered, with clothing, papers, magazines, cardboard boxes, fishing equipment. I perch on the edge of it, trying not to look at his cigarette.

At one end of the room there is a baby grand, next to long mullioned windows through which I can see two horses cantering in a field; their coats flash and gleam. At this end there is a bureau with photographs. Two children, a boy and a girl, at various stages of their school careers. To one side of the fireplace there is a small shelf with a wedding photo: your man, several years thinner and with more hair, next to a glowing blonde. But apart from Dan the house seems deserted. Holiday, I think. But my instincts are telling me I've walked into the middle of a troubled story.

Just for a change.

Dan shifts some papers to the floor and there is a clatter of something beneath them but he doesn't look.

– So you're – ?

– Louise Kenworthy – Susan's daughter.

– And your mother and my father were – ?

– Cousins.

– Right. How is your mother?

– She died.

Dan rubs his forehead.

– Oh – right. I did know that. Sorry.

– That's all right, I say.

– She couldn't have been that old.

– Sixty-nine. She had cancer.

– Oh, right. Yes, I remember now. Sorry.

I feel that the conversation is taking a downward turn. – Well, now I'm looking into remoter connections, I say lightly. – Seeing as my close family are all used up.

Dan leans back smoking and sizing me up. I produce the album.

– You don't live here, do you? he says suddenly.

– I've come up recently. From London.

– You've moved here?

– I'm renting. I brought this, just to see if you recognize anyone.

He gets quite interested as I go through the album with him.
– That's my dad as a little lad . . . well, well . . . I haven't seen that one before. We've got that one somewhere. That's my great-grandmother – yours too . . . well, well, fancy that. Do you want a brew?

Brewing up he becomes expansive. His old man died a couple of years ago, in his early seventies (what a boundary the death of a parent is, making your own death suddenly real. Not quite seventy, I'm thinking, seventy-one, thinks Dan). His mother's still alive. Living near his brother in Leeds. He didn't know any other family locally. Except one. An old guy he'd met in the pub. They'd been standing at the bar together and the old guy had said to someone else, Well, my name's Frank Woodhouse but I don't chop trees.

– So we got talking, Dan says, bringing tea over. – I told him I was called Woodhouse too and we worked out the relationship.

Dan sits down next to me and picks up the paper on which I have etched the family tree.

– This is him, look, son of Maggie. Albert's first wife.
– You're kidding.
– No, look.

Miraculously he finds a pencil and writes in a surprisingly neat, small hand, *Frank* beneath the line leading down from Maggie and Albert.

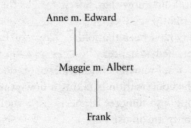

Anne m. Edward

Maggie m. Albert

Frank

– They weren't married long, Dan says, but she wouldn't give him a divorce. Both my dad and Evelyn were born before Albert could marry Jean.

Frank, son of Maggie, first wife of Albert. No picture in my mother's album, of course.

– Don't forget the other woman, Dan says. – Maybelline. The one he didn't marry.

Dan has obviously seen the newspaper cuttings too.

– Uncle Albert certainly got around, I say, and there is a flickering change in Dan's face.

– Yes, is all he says, and he inhales a lungful of smoke.

I have obviously hit the wrong note, so I go on, instead, to talk about Albert's parents, our great-grandparents, Anne and Edward, and turn to the photo I really want to know about.

– That's Anne, I say, and these are her sisters. But I don't know anything about them, do you?

Dan pulls the corner of his mouth down then taps the pencil against his knee.

– Wait a minute, he says. – We've got an album somewhere.

He gets up and leaves the room. I stay where I am, and for a moment am overcome by the strangeness of being here. My parents and Dan's, Lilian and Arthur, Albert, Edward and Anne, and all the generations before them producing this moment here, in which Louise Kenworthy sits in the lounge of her second cousin, Dan Woodhouse.

– Called to the bar at twenty-three, my mother used to say about him regularly, as if he'd been made pope. Brother Tony runs an engineering firm in Leeds and is, by all accounts, a self-made millionaire, though it was their father, Tom, who first recouped the family fortunes. Anyway, since moving back up the social scale they've had little to do with the rest of us. This doesn't bother me. I know how it works, without any intention, necessarily, on either side, just a smooth peeling away of paths. My mother didn't seem to resent it either, having that peculiarly Yorkshire combination of self-sufficiency and grudging respect for people who 'get on'. From time to time she reported things she'd heard about Tom's boys, as she always called them. Even the bad things were tinged with glamour, so that they never seemed entirely real. I always expected Dan to be a bit of a sharp-shooter, a high-flying, up-market wide-boy, snazzily dressed, smile like a TV presenter, not overweight and run-down, in a stained tracksuit. The other image hasn't disappeared, but the new one is superimposed rather weirdly on to it, with the result that my overall impression is out of focus. By my reckoning he is about the same age as me, maybe a year or two older. I have weathered better, taken better care of myself.

When Dan reappears he is carrying a dusty, leatherbound album. He sits down heavily again, closer to me this time. He smells of cigarettes and faintly of sweat. There is a tomato-coloured stain on the front of his tracksuit.

– Some of these are Sandra's, he says.

– Sandra's? I say quickly, and again there is that flickering change of expression.

– My wife, he says.

He flicks through the photos without showing me. Black and white glimpses of chubby babies, weddings.

Towards the back of the album the sepia photos begin.

– That's Albert, he says, with my grandmother, Jean. That's their wedding photo.

A small group of people in dark clothes.

– There's Anne, Dan says pointing.

– No Edward, I say, and Dan shakes his head. – Perhaps he'd died by then, I think.

There is another woman next to Anne, older, dumpy. I check in my album.

– Does that look like one of the sisters? Dan says, and I bring my album closer to his. It does look like the oldest of the three. We check everyone else in the picture, but no one looks like they might be the youngest sister.

– Hang on, says Dan, and he takes the photo out.

There on the back in the spidery handwriting I recognize from my mother's album, are the names of the wedding party: Albert and Jean with Jean's parents, then there is Anne, and Millicent.

– Millicent, Dan says. – That rings a bell. I seem to remember Anne had a sister called Millicent.

Susan Millicent, I'm thinking, and feel a pang of annoyance towards my mother, who must have known the name of her great-aunt all along, but say only, You don't remember what the other one was called, then? And he shakes his head.

Despite myself I feel a little chilled. No one knows anything about the youngest sister.

– I wonder why she isn't there, I say.

Dan looks at me ironically. – Maybe she ran off with Edward.

I close my album.

– Well, I say, I'm sorry to have taken up so much of your time.

– No, no, he says. – I'm interested. Really. I'm just wondering whether Frank might know anything. Being of the older generation.

– Maybe.

At the moment I don't want to know any more.

– He's always in the Bull's Head, Friday lunchtimes, Dan says. – Maybe you should go. We could go together, if you like.

– What about Sandra? I say.

Sometimes I'm too quick for my own good, as my mother never tired of pointing out. Dan probably didn't mean it that way at all. His face has changed again, but all he says is, I haven't seen Sandra recently, in a restrained kind of way.

– I'm sorry –

– Forget it.

Moody, I think.

– Yes, well, I say, thanks again. Very much.

Pause.

– I'll see myself out.

As I'm going he says, You say you're renting?

– That's right. Up at Shaw Cross.

– Does that mean you're not staying long?

I shrug. – It depends.

Dan nods.

35

– Well, as far as I know, Frank lives that way too. Blackshaw.
– Thanks.
– You're welcome.

CHAPTER 6

Martha

One day, nearly three months after her wedding, Martha's sisters came to visit. Millicent was first to the door, her homely face beaming and her figure so rounded with her third child that Martha could hardly get close enough to hug her. Anne came briskly in behind.

– What a smoke there is on the streets! My skirts are quite soiled. I don't know how you get used to it after the country. And such a smell!

Martha sank to her knees. – Who's this? she said, for there, clinging to her mother's skirts, was Millicent's older daughter, Eveline.

– She wanted to come, Millicent said, and now she's nesh.

Martha smiled at the old word, and looked into Eveline's eyes, which were a muddy grey, a shade or two darker than her own. Old, old eyes they were; there was nothing so old as the eyes of a child – Martha had noticed that before. It was as if you could look into them and see the origin of life.

She stood up abruptly, holding Eveline's hand. – Shall we go up? she said, and Eveline's greyish, elderly eyes looked more wary than ever, but she nodded.

– We couldn't bring the other two, said Anne. We'd have been driven daft in no time with Albert yammering on. And the journey was too long for Laura – how do you stand that noise?

Men were working opposite on the new glue factory, hammering and sawing. There was the clash of metal, and a fire engine suddenly blared past.

– Charles had to have premises near the city, Martha said, and she led them up the iron staircase that connected the shop floor to the other two storeys.

– Oh, I daresay it is good for business, Anne said, and she surveyed the little room that acted as parlour so that Martha couldn't help but see its shabbiness. Charles seemed to have no eye for the beauty of a place, but Martha had been making improvements. She had found a box of old prints, paintings of foreign places, and had decorated the walls with them to disguise the blue and chocolate wallpaper. She had spread a crocheted shawl of her own over the horsehair sofa to hide the worst stains. And there were decorative items in the room already. She took them down to show Eveline: shells and painted eggs, a stuffed bird and an antique globe. So although the room was dark, and never quite free of the smell of boiled greens and stored apples (she could hardly open the windows and let in great blasts of grimy air), Martha had persuaded herself that it was not without interest, it had a kind of shabby artistry. Unfortunately, this impression swiftly disintegrated beneath Anne's destructive glance.

– Well, I must say I'd miss my country walks, Anne said, seating herself on the sofa. – And you look as if you could do with some fresh air. She's looking pale, isn't she, Mill? Unless there's another reason, she added slyly, and Martha took the hats away while Millicent said mildly, It's a bit early for that, surely.

– Not so, I wish it was so, said Anne, sinking back.

Martha settled Eveline in the corner with a tray of shells and said quickly, I'll bring us some tea.

– Won't your servant bring it? Anne said, but was silenced by a warning look from Millicent.

Fussocks, Martha thought, but she said only, Would you like a cup of tea? to Eveline. – And a cake?

The child looked at her mother, unable to answer. She had a long, drooping nose, and an unfortunate habit of keeping her mouth open as if she couldn't breathe properly any other way. This caused her to sniff continuously, and to look gormless, as Anne often said.

Now Anne said, What's op? Theau'rt sollit as a box, and Millicent laughed merrily and said, Don't be frit of your aunt Martha, and they all laughed, and Martha went to the kitchen to put the great kettle on to boil, and a little pot for Eveline. Then she set out the apricot fritters and little tarts she'd been preparing all morning on the rosewood table that was the best item in the room, though badly scarred. She had covered it with doilies so that she would not have to be reminded of how Charles had scarred it.

– Where is Charles? Millicent said, and Martha explained that he had gone to address a meeting of the Vegetarian Society.

– They want him to stock their books, she said, pouring weak tea for Eveline.

– Vegetarians! said Anne. – There's a woman at church forever going on about the virtues of vegetarians and how healthy it all is, and her and her husband both as white as pudding cloths.

– The same cannot be said for Edward, Millicent said, sly in her turn, for Edward was a florid man of prosperous appetite. Anne laughed.

– Oh, but Edward's fair clemmed, you know, she said. – A mere scrannil of a fellow.

After that things went well enough, the talk all turning to children. Martha asked about Albert, and Laura, Millicent's younger child.

Albert was a limb, Anne said, and would be the death of her. Then she said, in a new tone, that she certainly hoped the new one would be less trouble.

– Anne! cried both sisters together.

– Another baby!

– When?

And Anne sank back as if she didn't know what all the fuss was about and said not for a long time yet, July or August. She just hoped if it was another boy he would be less trouble than Albert, otherwise she would just as soon have a girl.

– Especially one like Laura, she said. Just to look at Laura made you want to pick her up and hold her.

Martha looked at Millicent and Millicent smiled at Eveline. Anne was suddenly conscious of the girl.

– You're that quiet! she said. – I hardly think you're there.

Eveline looked startled and wary. Anne said she wished she had a child like Eveline, so quiet and helpful, not forever yammering and mithering like Albert. Eveline sniffed, then with a sudden movement knocked over her tea.

Martha and Millicent rushed over.

– No, no, Mill, said Martha. – Leave it be, and she fetched a cloth for the floor while Millicent mopped down Eveline, chiding her softly all the time. Martha scrubbed the rug, noticing at the same time how large and unwieldy the child's hands were, with big, reddish joints. Then she looked up and saw that Eveline herself was red to the roots of her hair, the way Martha herself blushed, her eyes desperate.

– Nay, lass, never fratch, she said, blushing herself, for Charles didn't like her to speak that way. She smiled at Eveline and took the cup away, and Anne launched into a description of the number of things Albert broke, and how, at Martha's wedding, he had completely mullycrushed Anne's dress with his jammy fingers.

The great kettle finally boiled, and Martha set out the teapot and little cups that were part of the set her father had given her when she married. She thought how typical it was of Anne to talk about a child as if it was deaf. Brawson, kalling bellweather, she thought. What she said was true, of course. Anne prided herself on only saying what was true. Both Laura and Eveline had their parents' features, but in Eveline the worst of them had combined (Arnold's great nose, Millicent's colourless eyes), and in Laura the best (Millicent's rosy complexion, Arnold's thick curls). Life was unfair, Martha thought, putting sugar into the little bowl. She herself had been told that she resembled the mother who had died when she was two. She also looked like Millicent, though Martha's features, unlike Millicent's, had in them the ghost of prettiness. She had thought, at one time, that that was why Charles had wanted to marry her. Anne was like their father, very fair, with a large chin, very fond of speaking her mind.

Martha wondered, briefly, what a child of hers and Charles's would look like, but then, though she had studied the big *Anatomy* in the shop, she couldn't see that the things Charles did to her at night would ever get her a child. But this was something she could never say, so she dropped the spoon with a clatter into the sink and carried the teaset through. She thought she saw Anne's assessing eye pass over it, but Eveline was whispering to Millicent, and Martha had to show them both down the stairs and across the slippery yard, where a wintry sun shone through a sooty filter, and flakes of soot drifted down like the first flakes of snow. That was what she couldn't get over, when she first moved to the city: not being able to see the sky.

– Oh, I could not abide a skulking child like that, Anne said, when Martha returned. – Sniff, sniff sniff – did you hear her? And chuntering on to herself.

Martha looked at Anne properly for the first time, and saw that she was ageing. There were fine lines on the plump white skin, and a mole with fairish hair on it on one cheek. Anne had aged, for all her pride, and Millicent too, returning with Eveline and smiling all over her wrinkled, rosy face. She, Martha, was here in this room with her two ageing sisters. One day there would be no one in the room, and then no room. But that thought was unreal. She poured their tea with deft movements, then sat in her chair with her hands neatly folded on her lap.

– We are mortal so that we might know infinity, the vicar of St Malachi's had said. He had said it in a hushed, impressive way, as though infinity manifested itself regularly before him, as though before his eyes was not the congregation, but stars and whirling nebulae. Martha liked to hear him talk, though many didn't, because he spoke things she had often thought, and made her see pictures in her mind. Now that she could no longer see the stars for smoke from the city, she thought of them often, and how, on the night she knew she would marry Charles the whole sky was blazing above the moor. She thought of them then, the stars and galaxies, whirling in their great orbits as she herself whirled, out on the moor, round and round with her arms flung out until she dropped. They were indifferent to her, and that made her feel better, as if nothing she did would matter very much. But they must all whirl round something, she'd thought. Every wheel has a hub. She'd asked her father and he had said that the earth went round the sun.

– But what does the sun go round? she'd said, and he didn't know. But in her own mind it seemed to her that everything, suns and galaxies, whirled round some indescribable blackness, that at the centre of all things there was nothing. It was not impossible to think of nothing, though she had read somewhere that it was. It was like the nothing that was there when you closed your eyes, only more so. And it was not frightening. But it altered everything.

The vicar of St Malachi's did not think that nothing was at the centre, he thought God was. He said that it was possible to believe in a conscious, loving God, because if people were both conscious and loving it had to come from somewhere. Martha held on to that thought, and took it out sometimes to examine it, though really, when she thought harder, she could only believe in the Nothing. Perhaps the two things were not different, she thought, and she thought all these things while sitting in a composed kind of way, looking at her sisters, for contemplating infinity seemed to take no time at all.

– Shall you be moving soon? said Anne, and Martha said, No, we have everything we need.

– Yes, but it is so small, said Anne. – All right for the two of you, but – She stopped expressively, and again Martha had the sense of her taking everything in, from the musty cretonne of the curtains to the marks on the little table that the doilies couldn't quite disguise.

– There is an attic, she said, and offered to show them, suppressing as she did so a nervous qualm. But Charles wasn't there, and Anne was eager, so they all went up the iron stairs again with Millicent holding on to Eveline as if afraid that they might give way.

It was a large, low, rambling room, the size of all the little rooms on the first floor. The ceiling bulged here and there and the floor was uneven, full of unexpected slopes and declivities.

There was no window, so Martha carried a lamp, and its light threw huge shadows around the walls. Their own outlines were projected there like great, ghostly giants.

This was where Charles kept his valuable books, his Voltaire and Berkeley, and the ones that turned out to be less valuable than he'd thought. She had heard him talking up here, to someone, voices raised in furious argument, and on one occasion at least she had heard terrible, strained cries.

– Leave me alone for the love of God.

– Once, once is enough.

But the voices had calmed down, and no one had come out of the attic, and by the time she had finished some talk or other Charles was back in the shop, with that sunken, inwards look on his face, which meant that she wasn't to approach him, or ask.

– See, Anne, there's plenty of room up here at any rate, Millicent said, and Anne sniffed and said it could do with a good dusting.

– Oh, Charles wouldn't like it, Martha said, and she turned, feeling a prick of anxiety between her shoulders. – Come, Eveline, she said (Charles had told her always to say come, rather than come on), and she caught the little girl's hand. – I'll show you how to make a button necklace for your dolly.

And she led them all back down the stairs, and brought out a little box of buttons and some thread. Eveline's eyes lit up warily then she smiled.

– I taught you to do that, Millicent said fondly.

Anne told them that she and Edward were to move in the spring to a house with large gardens and not one but two staircases leading from the reception room. And there would be a suite of rooms on the ground floor for Edward's mother, Mrs Woodhouse, who was getting a bit kegley on her pins. – I daresay we'll entertain grander company there, she said, with satisfaction. – But both of you must come as well, and Millicent laughed aloud.

Martha carried the pots back through to the little sink. She glanced at the window she never opened, through which it was barely possible to see because of the rills of grime. Out there, in the coal-black streets of Collyhurst, furnaces roared, pistons pumped and the fumes from oil rose with the steam. In the factory yards and wastelands low fires were lit, one-storey shacks with broken windows were piled upon the banks of the river, which ran slowly in many colours. There was the beating of hammers, the crying and swearing of many workmen, and even in summer, in the smoke-filled streets, people came and went like blackened wraiths.

Suddenly Martha wanted her sisters to go. It was always the same when she was with them, as if no time had passed and she would always be the baby. She heard them laughing now, over something Anne had said, laughing at her maybe, and it was as though all the black, poisonous vapour of the streets was rising in her own soul, swarming upwards like a cloud of bees into her head, stinging and worriting, until she was dinged and flited into a mizzy.

CHAPTER 7

Louise

A series of frames, people grouped together, told to smile – what do photographs have to do with anything, really?

It's not as if Dan looked at the photo and cried, God, you could be twins. As far as I know, I'm the only one who's ever noticed the resemblance. And I'm kidding myself, I've decided. Resemblances are easy to find, hard to prove. Look at the way people read dead relatives into a baby's face.

I tell myself these things while digging out a particularly intractable clump of nettles, using a trowel and gloves loaned to me by Mary. (– Needs a good weeding, that garden, Mary said. – I'll fetch you a trowel.)

I suppose it is passing the time. I never knew there was so much time, or that it could be so hard to pass. I've decided against looking Frank up, because I don't want to be trapped in some family net. But it's hard to think about things other than myself. I'd forgotten the way these broad, open spaces drive you back into the narrowness of your own mind.

Memories rise from the debris of forgotten things. On a hot day I'm suddenly cold, on a cold day, burning. They return as if time doesn't exist; as if the years between the girl I was then, doing something stupid/painful/vicious, and the woman I am now, watching the green curl of a caterpillar on a leaf, never happened. I am raw and shaking. It's like being pushed through a door in my mind to a different, appalling place.

Usually I'm in a hurry, or in a crowd, or both, and this doesn't happen unless I wake up in the early hours alone. Is this why people come to the country? Is this what's meant by 'finding yourself'?

Maybe I'm better off lost.

If I make an effort I can concentrate on what is actually around me now, the new frilly leaves of ragwort, the spikes of thistles, but the past seeps like water into the present.

Jamal, I think to myself, his name was Jamal. And when he was in the same room as me I had to touch him, and when he lay next to me in bed I had to put out my tongue and taste the bitter flavour of his flesh. His name was Jamal and I should not forget to use it, I should make my tongue say the word.

But the past is the past, I tell myself. I am Louise Kenworthy the popular and successful, liked at work by both junior staff and management, looking on a good day a good ten years younger than I am.

With a mild shock I realize I'm actually talking to myself, and stop immediately. I stand carefully, memory fading as a blow fades, and concentrate on another leaf, which is spatulate, with fronds.

Why wasn't the youngest sister at Albert's wedding? I suddenly think.

With mild annoyance I register the tooting of a car.

Wanker, I think, as it sounds off again. Finally I go to the edge of the garden and look down to the road below.

It's Dan.

– I'm just going to the pub, he calls up. – Frank'll probably be there. Are you coming?

I hesitate, peeling off gloves, wiping my hands on my jeans, then signal to him to wait, hurry indoors for my bag, pause briefly by the fragment of mirror in the kitchen, then pull lipstick lightly across my mouth.

It's a very nice car. Mercedes convertible. Obviously we don't use the Range Rover on Fridays. Even so, I pause before getting in, feeling a tremor like a small pain at the prospect of being driven. I lean back warily. It's like sitting in an armchair.

There is nothing to say. I watch the landscape streaking past.

When I look ahead there is the illusion of not moving, but to either side fields and trees stream past in flashes of green and yellow light.

She never saw it like this, the youngest sister, I think. The world with all its timing altered, distances foreshortened.

– You're not working up here, then, Dan says, breaking the silence.

– I've taken time off.

– What is it you do?

– I'm a fashion buyer.

His gaze flickers over me in the mirror. I'm used to this. I say I'm a fashion buyer, there is that quick, assessing look. In fact, I'm wearing a shirt and jeans.

– What about you – you're not working?

– Leave of absence.

– Oh.

I should probably ask why, or make sympathetic noises at least. But I don't want to know. And I don't want to answer questions myself. I'm beginning to wonder why I'm here.

Both of us seem tense in the car. I watch him narrowly. He has a different tracksuit on, washed this time, but the stubble is still there.

Dan, I think. Dan the man. Looking on a good day a good ten years older than he is. He catches me watching and I look quickly away. Try and fail to see my hair in the mirror.

In the pub it's different. Dan knows everyone: Pete, Jim, Dave.

– Saw you Sunday, Al, pretending to fish.

– I notice Bert's Boy got thrashed again in the three thirty.

We get to the bar, above which there are several sepia photographs of Old Broadstones. This pub, unlike the Boat, has gone for Tradition: log fire, oak beams, brasses. There is a picture of the workhouse over the bar.

– What'll you have? Dan says, and I order a diet tonic water, which seems to amuse him. He orders beer. – Will you have something to eat?

I haven't come out for a free lunch – I've got food in, having finally found the Co-op. But here, I understand, the rules are different. Dan is a different man. I can imagine him at that other bar.

– Well, just a sandwich.

– You're sure?

– Quite sure.

I sit down in a recess, among an array of brasses and photographs of the Old Smithy, and study the menu. Eventually Dan joins me and lights up. He's going to smoke throughout lunch, I can tell. I wonder whether to join him or whether, having refrained from buying more cigarettes myself, to object.

– Eh, John, he says, to a young man walking past. – How's the littl'un?

– Oh, he's fine, Dan, he's great.

– Is he walking yet?

– Walking? He's playing football!

– Best get him signed up, then, Dan calls after him, laughing. – I hear United are recruiting juniors. He turns to me. – He's crazy about that kid, he says.

I smile.

– Never stops talking about him. You'd think he was the first child to ever sit up or burp. Do you have kids? he says suddenly, though I'm sure he's taken in my ringless state.

– No.

– Best way, he says, drawing deeply on the cigarette. – Do you smoke, by the way?

He holds out the packet. I hesitate, then say no. Then stare, fascinated, at the beautiful blue ribbon of rising smoke. Dan doesn't seem to notice. He starts telling me about his kids, as I knew he would. Melanie is seventeen, musical, trained on the piano but now prefers the violin. Mark plays football. It looks as though he will follow his dad into law.

We order our food: a tuna steak sandwich for me, steak tartare for Dan. Dan's face is all closed up, he is looking away.

– Where are they? I say cautiously.

The kids are with Sandra in Spain, Sandra is with Luís.

– She just took them out of school, he says, and his small, rather hard blue eyes are all bewildered pain. – Right after the exams. Didn't wait for the end of term. Lured them out with tales of sun and sea and sand. And sex, of course. Not to forget the sex.

He ends bitterly and I await invective, having done this many times before, been the listening ear for the damaged male. When I open my mouth the right words automatically come out: She can't do that, can she?

– She can't keep them there, no. I'm waiting to see what happens after the holidays. I mean, Mel's got her A levels, for Christ's sake.

He drains his glass. – It's typical of Sandra, he says, planting it back on the table with some force. Running after some harebrained idea – never mind the casualties along the way. She wants a divorce, you know. Just like that – no discussion – twenty years swilled down the nearest drain. She wants me to put the house on the market, thinks she'll clean me out along the way – but she's got another think coming. By the time I've finished she won't know what's hit her.

This is all very unattractive. I'm saved from having to look sympathetic by the arrival of the food. Mine is on an enormous plate with chips.

– I can't eat all this, I say, dismayed.

– Of course you can, says Dan. – Get it down you. He goes off for more drinks.

The roast tuna is very good. I break the baguette into pieces and prepare to be more sympathetic. I should be more sympathetic, though there are two sides to every coin, as my mother always said. And I can't help remembering tales of his activities in a lap-dancing club in town. Even so, to come home one night to a message on the answerphone, which is how he says it happened, is devastating enough to deserve some sympathy. And all this is very recent. Whenever his one-of-the-boys act slips I see that incredulous, blasted look. The one I must have had a few months ago. So I scrutinize the photographs around us – the Digging of Greenbridge Tunnel, Quarry Workers, 1907 – and try to think up a diversion for when he returns.

– I knew about it, of course, he says, before I can come up with one. – She went out there after Christmas on one of these mid-season breaks – she was always saying we never went on holiday so I said she could go on her own if she liked. More fool me. She gets back and can't wait to go again. So off she goes at Easter and this time she doesn't come back. The next thing I know she wants a divorce. And she's saying that the house is *hers* and she wants me out. That's why she wants the kids with her, not out of maternal devotion – Sandra has all the maternal instincts of a cuckoo. No. As long as they're with me I have the right to the house. Once I'm out she can sell the place to raise money for her Spanish waiter. Over my dead body. No thought for where I'm going to live. Dig myself a hole in the ground for all she cares . . .

It must be hard, I think. Having to move out of that house to one only, say, four times the size of mine. Plus it's quite likely the house is Sandra's. My mother always said Tom's boys made money after marrying it.

– She won't get away with it, he says.

– Is that Frank? I say, nodding towards someone who couldn't possibly be.

– Where? says Dan. – Oh, no. Frank's a lot older. In his seventies. He's usually here by now.

– Maybe he's gone to a different pub.

– I shouldn't think so – he's a regular.

Dan looks at his watch.

– We'll give him a few more minutes. You're not in a hurry, are you?

– No, I say, annoyed.

– Want a pudding?

– No, thanks.

He orders more drinks. I think about him driving.

– Well, he says, enough about me. What about you?

– We don't want any insurance.

– It's not the insurance, June, says Frank.

– We've got enough to bury us both, says June. – That's all we want.

Frank reappears in the kitchen doorway, starts to say something then changes his mind and goes back into the kitchen shaking his head. June leans even further forward in her chair so that I fear she will fall off, and directs her peering gaze at me. – Is it time to go? she says, in a sepulchral whisper. I glance at Dan.

– All right, June? he says clearly. – We're just paying a visit. Nothing to worry about. Louise here's part of Frank's family.

– Family! June practically spits and shrivels back in her chair. Frank comes in with a tray.

– Don't mind June, he says, sitting on the arm of her chair. – How can I help?

About an hour and several albums later we have established that Frank has eighteen cousins on his mother's side, a batch of them Mormons in Utah. One cousin, Jesse, went to Australia and became a famous medium, and one of his uncles ran a travelling fair.

Of course, Frank would know more about his mother's side.

– Do you remember your father at all? Dan says at last.

– I was just trying to think, says Frank. – I don't *remember* him as such – I was only a babby when he left. I saw him from time to time after but not much. We read it in the paper when he died.

If there is any bitterness towards his father's family it doesn't show. He picks up all the albums except for one and puts them on the sideboard.

All this time June has been quiet. But as Frank moves the albums she leans forward again, towards Dan this time, and mumbles queerly.

– Sorry, June, Dan says. – What was that?

– Are – you – giving – her – one? she says, making an obscene gesture with her withered arm, and indicating me.

I don't have the kind of complexion that lends itself to blushes, but am interested to see that Dan has. This veteran of criminal law and lap-dancing clubs is blushing like a bride.

Frank hurries over, his lips pressed together. – Now, June, he says, and he sits down on the arm of the chair again and strokes her hair lightly until she subsides, dozing. But when Frank says, I did think I had some photos hereabouts – my mam left them me, she wakes up again suddenly.

– *Bitch*, she says, and we look at her in alarm, thinking she might mean me.

– Nay, now don't start, Frank says. – They never did get on, he explains to us. She had a bit of a temper, our mam, he says, raising his voice slightly for June, but she never meant any harm.

June's face wobbles in a temper of its own, her dim eyes suddenly clear.

– You didn't have to live with her all day, she says.

Frank laughs for our benefit and pats June's hair. – Now, now, these people haven't come to hear all this, he says. He carries on stroking her hair and soon June crumples against him. As Frank goes back to the book we can hear her raucous breathing.

– Now, then, here we are, he says. – I knew there was a wedding photo somewhere.

He shows us the photograph. It is spotted with age, but it is definitely Albert, round-faced and fair, looking very young. Next to him is a sharp, angular woman, about half Albert's size but older, dark hair tightly coiled.

– That's my mother, Maggie Durkin, Frank says.

I look from the picture to Frank. If anything he resembles his mother, tiny and dark, but with all the angles gone. On the next page there is a photo of Albert with two older women.

– Anne, I say. And isn't that –

– Auntie Millie, says Frank.

He knew Auntie Millie quite well. He had stayed with Anne three times in the big house, once for a holiday and once when he was very young, after Albert left Maggie for Jean. The third time was when Albert left Jean, returning briefly to the infamous Maybelline. For once mothers and grandmother were united in outrage. For while Anne never thought Maggie good enough for Albert, Maybelline was a dancer in a club.

– He'd been with her years, though, Frank said. – Cora's older than the lot of us.

– Cora? I say.

– Cora and Victor – Maybelline's two by Albert. He could only have been a lad. Maybe that's why he couldn't marry her. She was a lot older. But he kept going back.

Feeling lost in all this I get out my pencil and notebook, to make more scrappy diagrams of my family tree.

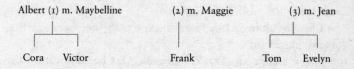

Albert (1) m. Maybelline   (2) m. Maggie   (3) m. Jean

Cora   Victor   Frank   Tom   Evelyn

– I wonder what happened to Maybelline, Dan says.

– Ah, well, now, I do know that, says Frank. – She went off to Canada eventually with Cora and Victor, and married someone from the armed services. That's all I know.

My family tree is rapidly becoming more tangled. Like a bush.

But Frank does remember Auntie Millie, because while he was there, at the big house in Sheffield, she visited several times.

– She was a nice lady, he says.

I lean forward.

– Anne and Millicent, I say, had a younger sister. I have a picture of her in my album – I should have brought it with me. You don't know her name, do you?

Frank pulls a thoughtful face. He has one of those rubbery faces that make any expression a caricature of itself.

– No, I don't know about any other sisters, he says. I do know my gran's maiden name, though – Hopkins. She was Anne Hopkins before she got married – Millicent would have been Millicent Hopkins. And they all lived around here then, though I don't think they were from round here originally.

Hopkins, I think. I take out my notebook and begin writing things down.

– There's a family grave, you know, Frank says. – Not here – Stockport way. That's what makes me think they weren't all from round here. My gran was buried in it. We went to the funeral, though my mam and her hadn't spoken for years. They fell out over money. But I think my mam was hoping to be remembered at the end, like. She was out of luck, though.

He smiles and his face is a pantomime of sadness.

– Anyhow we went. But it wasn't round here. She wanted to be buried with her mother. Cheadle way.

– Cheadle Hulme, June says unexpectedly, her head darting forward like a bird's.

– Nay, it wasn't, says Frank. – Cheadle. Or Cheadle Heath. That way anyroad. Have you thought of trying Somerset House?

Records aren't there any more, Frank, Dan says, and he explains where they are. All I can think about is the girl, growing up round here, perhaps playing where I played. I can feel a headache coming on.

– Why don't you try the library? Frank says. – They've got a good local history section.

Forget it, I think. I don't want to get obsessed.

– A good dialect section anyroad, says Frank. – Now, you say you're both born round here? But can you tell what I'm saying? Theau'rt middlin swipple o' thoose lung legs o' thine, owd cock o' mi cote.

We have to admit that we can't.

– No, not many can, these days. But I bet your mother'd've known, he says to me. – Or your father, he says to Dan.

We glance at one another smiling. But Frank fixes his mild, slightly prominent eyes on me intently.

– Those that grow up and leave lose touch with all that, he says.

– And they don't know what they're losing. They think it's all words, just words, that's all.

I glance at Dan and Dan shifts forward in his seat.

– Well, Frank, you've been a great help, he says.

– Not me, says Frank. – I couldn't tell you what you wanted to know. But I tell you what, he says, if you fancy going back to the Bull next Thursday, there's a dialect evening on.

Dan looks at me and I look at the floor.

– Well, that's nice, Frank, he begins.

– Poetry and recitation, says Frank, featuring yours truly. And a few other folk that don't want to see the old words disappear. You must come as my guests, he says, waving away our objections. – It's a good do.

We thank him and let him see us to the door. He detaches himself carefully from June, who seems to fold up behind him like washing. All the time we've been talking it's been raining, there are streaks of rain on the window next to the door. Through it I can see branches of broom, its pale blossom almost blown away, black seed pods forming. Far away a church clock strikes four, then the little clock on the wall.

– Thanks for all your help, I say.

– My pleasure, he says. – I never get to talk much about my dad's family.

– You don't mind being reminded about it, then, I say, thinking of the raw deal he's had, but he waves a hand.

– Oh, no, he says. – Life goes on, and he waves his hand again airily, as if conducting time. – My dad was very young, he says. – We all do daft things when we're young.

We step over tangled roses, their heads full of water, past the broom at the gate.

– Be seeing you, Dan says, and,

Next Thursday, says Frank, eight o'clock, and he smiles at us from the doorway, though I feel he is smiling at me, then he goes back in to June.

There is a little ginnel next to the house. Through it, a little way off, I can see a small park, swings and see-saw, parents and children gathering on it after school.

Dan opens the car door. All these amputated families, I think, as I get in. My parents dead, and Dan's father; Frank cut off from the rest of the family. Who else is there to ask?

– We could always try finding that graveyard in Cheadle, Dan says.

– Cheadle Heath, I correct him.

– Or Cheadle Hulme.

We laugh. Dan pulls out into the road. I sit back, wondering if Anne's little sister was already off the scene by the time Albert left Maggie. The thought depresses me.

– I wonder what happened to Maybelline, I say aloud. – You know, I remember calling a doll Maybelline. I must have heard the name somewhere and liked it. I don't suppose my mother was too pleased.

– I daresay Cora and Victor are still around somewhere, he says.

– I daresay. Now I don't like those names at all.

Keep it light. Keep it light and chatty all the way home.

The rhododendrons on the path to the cottage are bowed with rain. They brush the roof of the car, sssh-sssh, sssh-sssh.

I realize I don't want to ask Dan in.

– Look at this rain, I say, for the sake of saying something as we pull up. Large heavy drops are gathering force.

– It's supposed to be picking up next week, Dan says.

– Didn't they say that last week? I say.

– Maybe we could go for a walk, or a picnic, if it does pick up.

The offer hangs in the air. I think quickly, and to buy myself time, say, What about the evening at the Bull?

Dan laughs. I can see that an evening spent listening to people saying, Eh up and Aye at one another isn't his idea of a night out either.

– Well – we could do both, he says.

If I'm still here, I think. – We *could*, I say. – But I think we should go to Frank's evening. He did go to some trouble for me.

I get out of the car and Dan gets out with me, but remains holding the door. – Louise, he says, are you on the phone here? In case I come up with something, you know. I could give you a ring.

I hesitate, then scribble the number of my mobile on the back of his card.

– Next Thursday, then, he says.

I wave as he draws away, then hurry up the path before the downpour begins.

Inside I massage my aching forehead. What am I getting myself into? I think. Here I am, Louise Kenworthy, being drawn more and more into the family web. I can almost see it, large and fine like a spider's web, trapping me wherever I go.

Outside my window all the colours are glowing in the heavy light. The whole of the green, saturated world is glowing with mystery. If I look up now, on to Blackshaw Edge, I might almost expect to see the figure of a young girl, running and jumping on the open moor, arms flung wide.

CHAPTER 8

Martha

Beestings's best, better than afterings. Farmer give us beestings off cow that cauved, it were lovely, rich and thick, made beautiful curd tarts that clogged meauth.

Sowd horse and bowt donkey, that were Faither, jiggered op rump and stump.

– Faither, I says, we shall ha to fly op wi'th hens.

– Shut thi meauth, says Faither. – Theau'rt wur nur a clockin hen.

But first it wur four servants, then three then two. One bi one like Johnny Ringo's sheep. Good shuttance says I. But then there were only me. Mill and Annie both left and only me, askin farmer for milk and eggs, shame on me, Faither says, beggin like a cripple on a bridge.

– But what else? says I. – Hang yed like a pown heaund?

– Tell the truth an shame the devil, says I.

– Poverty's hard, hard as hell's hobstone, and life gets harder as you get older, Jess says, her that left last. I did all cookin and scrubbin and diggin for peat reaund our way.

– Not so as you'd notice, Faither says. A lick here and a spit theer, but all Faither could do was tek to bed, goin deaun like watter in a dych, and everythin in heause cracked as a workheause pot.

Still all things have an end and a puddin has two, and along comes Mr Ridgeley, owd friend o' Faither's and a cock on his own midden, as they say.

– Get thi best bib and tucker on, Faither says to me. – I'll have noan o' thi donkey looks.

And Mr Ridgeley brings his nephew, face long as a week's washin, never oppens his meauth, Faither tells me not to oppen mine, and so the deed wur done.

Deed's dun, get thi gun, no use skrikin, milk's all gone.

Me and Faither et like feightin cocks for days.

Then owd Mr Ridgeley cocks his toes and slips off catch, youngun gets shop and Faither says, Reight.

First cock o' hay fears cuckoo away.

So there I wur, nobbut sixteen year old, knot tied to a man who's queer as two cross sticks.

First thing is, the way I speyk won't do. I have to change it or stay eaut o' shop. I have to practise every day, speykin and spellin.

This way or that I never got much school. Weather bad, roads up, Faither ill. Mill taught me and sometimes Annie, but she wur always cranky side eaut.

Nowt but nits and lice in thi yed, says she. Now I have to keep it all in mi yed, for if I say mithered, or, I'll just sken books, to a customer, he gets in a reight fratch.

Sometimes I make him laugh. If he asks me what I think of someone and I say, He's nobbut a bell – wants hangin, or He's like fire – in and eaut, he'll laugh sudden, then next time be mad as a hen, there's no tellin. So I sit sollit as a box and practise thinkin before I speyk.

But marriage is hard work, there's nothin like the work that marriage is.

Killin hisself to keep hisself he is, and me with him. Two stummacks for work at least.

Up at six, light the fire that won't light with the flue all clogged and smokin, put on overalls and clogs, make dough for daily bread, make beds, dust and sweep.

Then I sort washin to be sent eaut. We rowed over that one. But even he saw it were dryin blacker in our yard than afore it wur done.

– You cannot get white meyl eaut of coal sack, says I, and he crimps all his lips up and walks off stiff as a poker.

Fridays beat carpets, Saturdays lead stove, back and forth, back and forth with my little black brick. Till we row over that as well, for my skin's soakin all black lead up and I look a reight mullock after, and even he sees I can't work shop like that. So I mither on and get a girl, a whey-faced pulin one, nose like a Halifax door knob. She does stove and winders once a week, be thankful for small mercies. Mondays bakin, Tuesdays ironin and mendin, turn collars reaund, never throw a shirt away, press it wi gosterin iron, mi own dress fallin apart, but what cannot be helped must be bided.

Wednesdays scrubbin.

Sometimes I look up from my scrubbin at the square winder that's all grimed over day after it's been washed, and I'm back on moor wi Mill, runnin yonder, flingin mi arms wide, gorse in summer then heather, shoutin out daft words to sky.

Moonpennies.

Nethercrop.

Mowdiwarp.

Shepster.

Then I'd cob a stone or shout after strangers, What are you gawpin at?, and Mill'd hopple up after, all eaut of breath in hutherin wind.

– Martha, you're growin op wild an ovish, you're wur nur a lad.

One day we saw children tekken op to workheause in that van like a horse box. Me and Mill held hands.

– Where are they takin them, Mill? Why?

I remember smell of new laundry after suddlin, better than new-mown hay. And lant, steamin in the lant jar, strong as horse piss.

Then I look again and I'm still swelterin in kitchen, fire switherin on and mi one winder black as grate. Even sun can't find Collyhurst, it's black as Devil's nuttin-poke.

I know where I am, I've died and gone to hell, all darkness and flame and soot and wraiths.

But a bellin cow forgets its cauve, and there's no use peauchin over slattered milk.

Soon I get so as I can watch this woman movin reaund shop, doin this or that, watch her hands, reddish, segs on them, watch her elbow move back and forth, back and forth, hear her thinkin before she speyks, yes sir, no ma'am, oh yes, ma'am, watch her walkin past him, all cack-handed and conscious as she goes, like she's dribbled deaun her front, him watchin her with his glinty eyes, and all the words she could ever say shrivellin up in her meauth.

CHAPTER 9

Louise

All right, I admit it, I am obsessed.

Here I am, in the library, going through census records. The records are on microfilm and I have been staring at the screen so long that all the names are flickering into one another.

Isaac Lob, tanner, Lees Lane, Jane his wife, James his son.

Hezekiah Locke, Lees Lane, Ruth his wife, Sarah and Joan his daughters.

I'm getting nowhere for the following reasons:

(a) the census is in street order, there is only a full name index for 1851.
(b) I don't have a full name for Anne's father, my great-great-grandfather.
(c) I don't have an address.
(d) I don't even know that the family were living here in 1851.

Frank seemed to think that they weren't from here originally, though maybe that was only the mother's side.

Because there were families called Hopkins living in Broadstones in that year. Eight of them, in fact.

> Abel Hopkins, postmaster
> Enoch Hopkins, smith
> Joseph Hopkins, publican
> Josiah Hopkins, carpenter
> Samuel Hopkins, thatcher

Seth Hopkins, chandler
Thomas Hopkins, cowbanger [whatever that means]
William Hopkins, hen gunner [ditto]

The librarian is very helpful, bringing me church records in an enormous file, the address of the nearest Mormon church, a leaflet on the Family History Centre in London. But without an address, a full name, I seem to be wasting my time.

And what am I doing here, really?

I sit back to give my eyes a rest, watch the librarian flitting round the shelves like a distracted owl.

Then, almost doodling, I sketch out what I now know of the family tree:

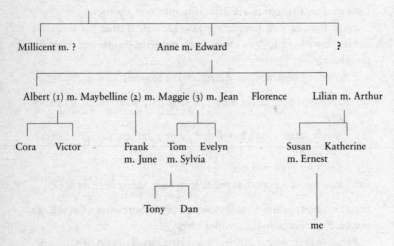

I've filled in a few spaces, found out a few things I didn't want to know. I could go on doing that indefinitely. I forgot to ask, for instance, whether Frank and June have any children. I could find that out if I wanted to, but I still can't find out anything about the youngest sister.

That's research for you. You can find out anything except the thing you want to know.

I stare at my family tree, as if willing her name to appear.

There is the sound of a child crying, petulant, repetitive, sawing through the threads of my consciousness. I look up but the mother is nowhere near. Then, before the librarian can do anything, there is an elderly woman bending over the little boy, talking to him in a low, low voice, so that his passion changes, and he listens to her saying, Such a big fuss, such a big fuss, over and over, very quietly. Then she takes out a hanky and dabs his wet cheeks and forehead. There is a look of deep attentiveness on his face, as though even his skin is listening where she presses it.

Then his mother hurries over and takes his hand in an embarrassed kind of way, barely saying thank you. The old lady steps back as they leave, and I look away from them, through the window, feeling quite stricken inside.

The afternoon is a moving pattern of light and shade. Light shivers through the long grass on the croft behind the library; beyond it, cars streak endlessly along the road, one, two, three, four, always going somewhere, people always have somewhere to go.

Even as I watch the light is changing, a woman in a red coat passes out of view, a swallow dips and rises, a scrap of paper drifts across the croft. One moment passes into another faster than anyone can measure, yet here am I, looking for the past.

I turn at the clatter of many books. There are exclamations of annoyance, and laughter. The librarian is setting up a display.

Helping her is a tall young man with black hair in a pony-tail; complexion slightly darker than olive. He is wearing a blue shirt and pale cotton pants. He looks nothing like a librarian.

When the boards are set up and the librarians gone, I make my way over. THE WORKHOUSE: 1601–1930 is the heading, and beneath there is a larger reproduction of the photograph in the pub, showing the main building sideways on. *The workhouse stands 1069 feet above sea level, on an exposed plateau above Broadstone Moss*, it says on a printed card next to the photograph. Other sheets of information are pinned to the surrounding boards.

LIVI MICHAEL

STAFF FOR THE YEAR 1872–3
Bernard Slater, Master of the Workhouse
Sarah his wife, Matron of the Workhouse
Jane Heywood, temporary nurse
Edith Jones, domestic servant
Harry Wilcox, stable hand
John Hanna, chaplain
Henry Hawkyard, Clerk to the Guardians

Next to this there is a photograph of the Guardians of the Poor, a hatchet-faced set if ever there was one. All the Great and Good of Broadstones without a smile between them, but then people didn't smile, did they, on old photographs? Each face has the seriousness of sepia, yellow-grey deepening to brown, the colour of the past itself.

Next there is

ANIMALS KEPT AT THE WORKHOUSE
13 COWS
1 bull
2 horses
5 pigs
20 sheep
one dozen fowl

– Excuse me, says the tall librarian, very close to my ear, and I step back as he pins up a further sheet. He has rolled up his sleeves and the hair on his arms is fine and dark.

FOOD BROUGHT FROM WAKEFIELD
Bread
Oatcakes
Rice
Tea and butter for the infirm

One Thomas Hawley, pauper, complained to the Board of Guardians about the milk, which was always sour, and there is a letter from Henry Hawkyard to the Inspector of the Poor, defending the use of whiting in the baking of bread: *I beg to state that whiting, being a soft chalk and a carbonate of lime, is commonly used instead of yeast in the making of haver cakes.*

On the next sheet there is a list of work undertaken by inmates:

> Cleaning, including the cow shed and byres
> Chopping firewood
> Digging peat moss
> Oakum picking (children)
> Fetching sand and pebbles from the quarry
> Breaking rock

In their time it seems that Hawkyard and Slater increased the amount of stone to be picked by male inmates from three to seven hundredweight a day.

Then there is

RECOMMENDATIONS FOR IMMEDIATE CHANGES TO BE MADE TO THE POORHOUSE ABOVE

BROADSTONES.

The stone-built outhouses have no ventilation.
There are no exits for fire.
There is no running water, hot or cold.
The wards for male vagrants are the worst of any district.
Six women and seven children sleep in a room 8′4″ by 9′10″ on plank beds with no pillows.
The sick are looked after by paupers, not nurses. One Jonah Williams (76) is in charge of the men's sickroom, and one female who has been lately discharged from an asylum in charge of the women's sickroom.
Those of unsound mind are lodged with the rest, mingling freely with the children.

> Robert Kennedy, Inspector, October Sixteenth, 1871

Beneath this is Henry Hawkyard's reply: that he is not in the business of encouraging vagrancy, that if he did the place would swarm over with professional tramps, that there was a great and increasing difficulty in hiring proper staff, witness his many attempts to hire a teacher for the children.

– He seems to have been a real sweetheart, I say to the beautiful librarian, who is still sorting out sheets.

– Hm?

I tap my chest.

– Heart of gold, I say, Esther Rantzen.

– Henry Hawkyard? he says. – Oh, yes. Any number of people might have killed him in the end.

He indicates the notice he has just pinned up. MURDER AT THE OLD HALL, it says. I stare at it in surprise. I have heard the story before but had never realized who it was.

– Paul, says the other librarian, telephone.

Paul, I think. I had thought he would have an exotic name. Like Jamal, I think suddenly, and a small pulse in my forehead quickens.

I turn back to the notice.

At 9.15 p.m. on the fifteenth of November 1891, Henry Hawkyard was sitting in his dining room whilst supper was being prepared. The cook, who was in the kitchen, was startled to see a man lurking by the scullery door, and at first mistook him for Worrall, the coachman, since his face was covered by a muffler. But the man crossed the kitchen swiftly and held a gun to her head. Breaking from him she ran from the kitchen to the hallway, leaving the maid to confront the intruder. The scullery maid was rendered motionless, but the cook, Nellie Flitch, ran on to the dining room.

'There's a man in the house,' she screamed, as the intruder, following, broke in behind her. Hawkyard grabbed the man's wrist while Mrs Flitch fled to the alarm. She then ran for help to the Liberal Club with the maid following after. A party of eight men who had heard the alarm were already hurrying up the hill. By the time they got to the Hall, Henry Hawkyard was lying in a pool of blood. He had been stabbed fifteen times.

My mother told me this story once. All the time I am reading I can hear echoes of her voice telling me that no one was ever convicted of the murder. *Truth will out but that one never*, she said.

Paul returns, carrying files. He leans in front of me, apparently oblivious, and pins up a photograph of Hawkyard: baggy, sagging face, full, downturned mouth, then an extra sheet which is the police report from the scene of the crime.

> . . . a quantity of blood on the floor of the kitchen, where the deceased was found lying; marks of blood on the scullery door, kitchen side, and on the door knob, and on the inside of the door. Two smears had apparently been made with fingers on the panel. Marks were in evidence on the scullery floor; there were blood marks on the slop stone, on the wooden rail beneath the window sill and on the wall at the side of the window. It is still not clear how he entered, as there was no sign of a lock being forced. In the dining room itself there were marks on the door leading into the hall. The blood had trickled down to the floor, a distance of 3′6″, and along the carpet to the kitchen where the deceased lay; the conclusion being that the deceased had dragged himself the length of the hallway . . .

I can feel myself shrinking from the words as I read them. It is as if a layer of skin has been stripped away and I can feel the thrumming of my own blood very near the surface. Even the flesh on the palms of my hands seems to shrink.

– Are you all right? says Paul.

Not as oblivious as he seems, then. I nod at him, looking away (but I can almost feel the wounds, the leaking of blood).

– The wonder of it is, Paul says quietly, very near to me, that he wasn't murdered years before. In fact, he'd been retired for some time when it happened.

He is looking at me quite intently now, and I feel a mild flow of heat.

– He did well for himself, I say, turning back to the board, if he could retire in the Old Hall.

– He did very well for himself, Paul says. – He made a lot of money out of what he did. One way or another.

– So you think it was someone from his past? I say, smiling.

– Probably, he says, and he is almost smiling. – But we'll never know. Will we?

I remain smiling, but I'm thinking, The past caught up with him.

– Why all this interest in him now? I say lightly.

– You haven't heard? he says, surprised. – The workhouse, and the land around it, are up for redevelopment. And there's a move to turn it into luxury homes.

I laugh, then see he's serious.

– Who? I say.

It is a joint venture, he tells me, between the council, its Enterprise Development Agency and a well-known local builder called Boyd, to convert the building, although there is opposition to this locally. Local feeling is that it should be kept as a heritage centre. In fact there's a meeting about it tonight.

– If you're interested, he says.

I stare at him, disconcerted. For a moment a small, unstable part of me, like a candle flame, wonders if he's asking me out.

– Tonight? I say, and he goes on to talk about the Residents' Association, and the strength of local feeling in Broadstones, that the council and property developers between them are tearing it apart. All the mills have gone, the Old Hall has gone. New buildings go up without anything being commemorated, just lost. And when you talked to people it wasn't what any of them wanted. The borough was changing all the time, but no one was listening to the people who live here. And the Tourist Board, who, one might think, would have a vested interest in preserving the heritage, only seem interested in more hotels and a marina.

All the time he's talking I watch the smooth brown of his skin, which becomes more pitted near the hairline, the quiver of a pulse in his throat. He is not from round here, I think, and I wonder absently where he might be from.

– So you're opposed to all this, I take it, I say, when he pauses.

He blinks at me as if I've just said something incredibly stupid.

– I'm opposed to the loss, he says. – And the waste. And the way no one listens to what people want. I think it's important for people to make themselves heard. To come to the meetings if they can. And get involved.

His eyes, which seem permanently attached to some inner vision, suddenly focus again on mine.

– Well – I don't live round here, I begin.

– Oh, he says, as if suddenly losing interest.

– But I was born here, I add swiftly. – I've just come up here from London to – to look into my family tree. Not with a great deal of success, I'm afraid. But, then, I haven't got much to go on. Just a few photographs. I know they lived round here, and I think they owned land originally, but I don't know where.

Paul frowns, attractively, and turns to the shelf behind. – These are the best books we've got on local history, he says.

I watch the movement of his arms as he picks up the books, the tensing of his shoulder muscles, the fullness of his thigh, which is flattened against the desk next to me. My eye rolls all over him like a marble in a marble run until I check myself. I'm too old for this, I tell myself. He's little more than half my age.

He passes four books to me, flicking through the last one before handing it over.

– You might find something in here, he says.

– Thank you.

Obediently I sit down with the books. All the time I'm reading them part of my mind is following his movements around the library. When he passes close to me I fear that this will be obvious, that if he looks he will see a sticky, glistening trail, like the track of a snail.

What am I – thirteen?

He will certainly be spoken for. I conjure up someone Nordic for him, athletic yet cultured. He might even be married. Or gay.

This thought makes me concentrate more fully on the books. I frown and rub my fingers against my forehead, read every sentence three times.

A lot has been written about land ownership and the division of land; about enclosures, which came late to Broadstones and went on throughout much of the nineteenth century. There is the selling of land by desperate farmers to lords who wanted to hunt and shoot; there is the death of the last lord of the manor and the division of his estate into twenty-odd parts. Rich men from the south bought it, built their own houses and claimed to be lords themselves.

But only Henry Hawkyard could afford to buy the Old Hall.

The story goes on, from one book to another: a long, degenerating tale of dispossession that kept the workhouse very busy throughout its last hundred years. Land values went down, people lost the right to pasture or to dig peat, as their neighbours did deals and put up walls. Bitter enmities ensued. To this day, to my knowledge, the Henshaws do not speak to the Harrops, the Buckleys to the Bradburys or Lockes. Mills lost land and closed, generations of young people grew up and left looking for work. The land was poor for crops, the climate worse. After the war it was said that you couldn't pay people to live here.

Then overnight, it seemed, all that changed. Now even a decent-sized shed, stone-built with a view, will be snapped up by property developers, converted and sold off for a small fortune. Not to locals, of course. None of the people who left could ever afford to come back now.

Who would want to come back? Just reading these books brings back the weight of the past, its legacy.

None of this is getting me anywhere. I flick through the pages, aware of the lines of branches across the window, a flash of sunlight.

An old man puts out a trembling hand to a bookcase and the movement is unexpectedly beautiful.

Life goes on, I tell myself. Outside, over there, through the window, round the corner, between bricks and paving stones the astonishing beauty of the world goes on. Everything that happens, is said or written, disperses gradually like light itself. Words and stories travel the world like dust.

Finally I come to a section on the workhouse. And the placing out of workhouse children in apprenticeships.

> Workhouse children formed the cheapest labour that a manufacturer could get. The demand for them was so great that thousands of them every year were placed in mills all over the country and thousands more transported to Canada.

> > Poor John High was an orphant boy
> > From the workhouse school he came.
> > His master Buckley beat him
> > Till he was blind and lame.

> Tom the devil flogged our backs daily till the blood ran freely down our legs, and then mill oil poured on the wounds that our clothing should not stick.

> Those who lived near Hollin Clough spoke of hearing the children scream all through the wild dark nights.

I sit and stare at the page.

The horror of history seems to seep upwards through it like a bloodstain.

Maybe it never disperses.

I flinch at a touch on my shoulder.

– Sorry, Paul says. – I just thought I'd bring you one of these.

A leaflet from the Blackshaw and Harrop Residents' Association, like the one in the hallway of my cottage the day I arrived, the one I threw away. About the meeting tonight.

– They'll be discussing the workhouse, Paul says. – I just thought you might like to know.

I gaze at him numbly. What can I say?

That I don't want to know at all? That this bleak history is part of the reason I left, wanted to leave, as soon as I could imagine any future?

But there is Paul with his oil-dark eyes, and there is the pull of all those lost people.

– I don't know, I murmur. – I'll try.

And Paul smiles, a heart-stopping smile, and moves away.

For several moments more I stare at my desk, feeling as though I'm staring at the ocean of the past, as though I've been trying to contain it in several pots and pans. And I'm still no wiser about my great-great-aunt.

Soon I realize that it's time for the library to close, that people are packing up around me in a way that makes it clear I should go. I've been here since lunch and have had no food. I stand up, pick up my jacket and bag, nod self-consciously at Paul as I leave.

I didn't ask him whether he would be at the meeting.

There is a commotion of starlings in the air as I stand on the steps. Already the shadows have lengthened, attracting the eye as much as the solid, real things, which seem less substantial and real as the light disperses. The colours of flowers, in hanging baskets or small front borders, are very pure.

I set off looking for a bus stop, because if I'm going to this meeting (which I'm by no means sure about) I will need to be quick. I walk past roadworks and lined-up traffic, terraced houses with for-sale signs, a new supermarket, an old church hall. This landscape is like a language, I think, but not one I can understand.

Traffic on the main road is clogged like a drain. I turn off it into a street in which all the windows burn with reflected sun. My steps feel weighted as if I'm dragging the oceanic mass of the past about with me in great nets.

All I wanted to do was to find out about one person. Now all I can think about is that endless stream of lost people pouring into that dark vault on the hillside.

Lost so that all records, all human memory of them, are lost. Lost so that even their genes, those faint but indestructible sparks of hope sent into the future, are lost.

Now, of course, they're all on the streets. That's progress for you.

All bus stops seem to have been moved, black bin liners tied carefully around the signs (who does that job, and why does no one ever see them?). I don't recognize anything on this street, and gradually I realize that the street never used to be here. This whole area is mapped out differently from when I knew it. Finally, round the corner I find a small, temporary stop. Another woman is standing next to it and she smiles cheerfully at me as I approach. I stand next to her, allowing the jumble of questions, who killed Henry Hawkyard, how can I find out my great-great-aunt's name, to settle in my mind. As I wait in this street I do not know for a bus that may not come, it occurs to me that if I do go to the meeting it will not just be because of the beautiful librarian, but because at least it is a place to be.

CHAPTER 10

The Blackshaw and Harrop Residents' Association meets in Mary Brennan's house. Mary Brennan lives in a red-brick semi that reminds me sharply of the house I grew up in, except that ours was council. There is an azalea and a straggly hydrangea to the front. The overall effect, net curtains, cracked earth instead of grass in the garden, is of a slightly weary shabbiness that makes my back straighten as I rap smartly on the door.

At least I have had no trouble getting here. I barely had time to slip on a loose jumper and eat some cheese before I caught sight of the bus on Shaw Road and bounded off to meet it in case there wasn't another one for a week.

I knock again on the door and finally it opens. Mary Brennan too is respectably shabby, plump and pigeon-shaped, elderly-looking though probably not yet sixty. She has grey-brown hair tucked behind each ear, horn rims.

– Oh, I'm sorry, she says, a tad breathlessly. – Come in, come in – so many people – were you waiting long?

She shows me into a large room, lounge and dining room knocked together, that is indeed full of people. And cats. Pink pot cats on the mantelpiece, window-sill and bookshelves.

– Sit down – do take a seat – Petra's taking the meeting – she'll be starting soon – coffee or tea?

Here I am, Louise Kenworthy, in a room full of people I don't know. I feel an unpleasant qualm as I walk into it, towards the most inconspicuous seat I can find. Once there I gaze carefully at the carpet, a series of brown and mustard squares, conflicting almost totally with the lilac walls.

Mary Brennan runs to and fro with orders for drinks.

– That's three coffees, two herb teas, an orange juice, one hot water and four ordinary teas.

– Can I give you a hand? says an elderly gentleman with a long, grizzled jaw.

Mary's eyes flit round the room like flies.

– *Would* you, Les, she says, that would be kind, and they disappear together.

I scan the room quickly but there is no sign of Paul. I glance behind just to make sure and a man I've never seen before grins and nods at me, revealing broken yellow teeth.

– Nigel Scowcroft, he says.

Uncertain whether or not to respond, I nod briefly and turn away.

At the front of the room an older woman stands. She wears stout boots and thick stockings. Her chest is thrust forward so that from the side she resembles a question mark.

– That's Petra Willis, Nigel Scowcroft hisses in my ear. I stare at his lean, withered face. Just my luck, I think. Instead of Paul I have Nigel Scowcroft.

– I think we should get started now, Petra says, cutting through the preliminary noise.

– Excuse me, Petra, says Mary Brennan, I just have to check. Was that two herb teas or three?

It is established that it's three.

– And – sorry, Petra – I just thought I'd mention, we do have peppermint as well as camomile, so which would you rather?

One opts for peppermint and the other, after a brief discussion (well, if it's not too much trouble – no, not at all) for camomile.

– Honey? says Mary Brennan, and at the front of the room Petra nearly skips with impatience.

Two people want honey, but only one of the herb teas. Then one man who had said he didn't want sugar changes his mind, and a youngish woman with long hair and arty leggings offers everyone sweeteners from her shoulder-bag, and the woman next to her with the mousy perm takes one.

– My name's Marie, by the way, says the woman with the leggings, smiling brightly at everyone.

Petra raps on the floor with her stick.

– If we *can* begin, she says, and Mary Brennan says, Of *course*, and apologizes several times, and backs out of the room almost curtseying, knocking over a pink pot cat on the way.

– Now, says Petra Willis, rustling papers in a managerial kind of way, let's get going, shall we? I'd like to welcome the people who are with us for the first time tonight. I formed this Association, she says, glaring at us all, because it seems to me to fulfil a very real need in this area. There is a *very great concern* about the level of *vandalism*, and I use the word advisedly, being perpetrated by industry and property developers, who between them are changing the nature of the area *irrevocably*, causing untold damage to the environment and the loss of our heritage, of which most people in Broadstones, incomers and natives alike, are justifiably proud. I'm sure you'll agree – you wouldn't be here otherwise – that hardly a single day passes in Broadstones without something, some treasured site, changing or disappearing for ever.

Murmurs of agreement all round.

– And I'm sure you're aware that feelings in the borough are running very high indeed. One question is uppermost in the minds of residents. Is Broadstones safe in this council's hands?

Scattered clapping and a few hear-hears. Petra raises her hand.

– There are several items on the agenda, she says, but first of all I'd like to introduce you to the people who've come to speak to us tonight. Two councillors out of all the ones I approached have kindly – some would say bravely – offered to come here tonight to try to answer any questions you may have. Irene Travis from the Planning Committee.

Irene Travis has a bony, discontented face and sharp blonde hair in a crew-cut. It is almost a brutal face. Councillor Norris has silvery hair and a knowing look. He smiles at me in an amused way as Petra introduces him.

– But first, Petra says, I'd like to introduce you to Miss Carol Paige, who works in our own local studies library, and who is going to talk to us tonight about the latest heritage site in Broadstones to be under threat – the workhouse.

It's the librarian. Not Paul, but the one who was so helpful when I was looking up my family tree. She is small, with fair, fluffy hair and a pink face that pinkens further as everyone turns to look. She must be here instead of Paul, I think, and feel a disappointed pang. She gets up, papers slipping from her knee, and makes her way to the front where Petra, now beaming, ushers her into a special seat.

Someone coughs into the silence that follows. Carol shuffles her papers, apparently unable to find her place. Then she begins.

– The old building – she says, and an elderly man at the front says, Can you speak up a bit, please?

– That's George, Nigel Scowcroft says in my ear. I shift my seat forward.

Carol begins again. – The old building, she says, much too loudly, was built in 1603 by William Booth of Booth Hall in response to the Elizabethan Poor Law, which assigned responsibility for the poor to parishes. The idea was that they would be usefully employed . . .

She goes on for a while, telling us things we already know, and I lean back and stretch a bit. All the waiting faces are yellowish in the yellow light.

– The original hall was a timber-framed wattle-and-daub mansion, she says, sounding like a tourist-information leaflet.

– After the Poor Law Amendment of 1834 it was rebuilt using stone flagging. It has the unusual feature of being built in the traditional Elizabethan E shape, with gabled ends, using local stone. That's unusual for workhouses, I mean, she says, looking up at last. – That's why it's a listed building.

No one says anything, so she goes on.

– And it has one other unusual feature – a copse of trees, mainly larch and spruce, thought to have been planted by the workhouse children.

People exchange glances now, the impact of this is not lost. In my own mind there arises the image of pale hands pressing seeds into the cold earth.

Irene Travis flicks cigarette ash into an ash-tray.

– It was in use continuously, Carol goes on, until 1935, at which time the estimated cost of restoration was four thousand pounds. But now the latest survey estimates costs at just over one million pounds.

Lots of indrawn breaths, and George bursts out, That's just what happened with the Old Hall, and several voices agree with him.

– They let it rot till the cost of doing it up was too much – then they knocked it down.

There is a small clamour of agreement.

– What I can't understand is, Les says, leaning forward, if it's a listed building no one's allowed to take it apart, are they? They've got to do it up as it was before – not turn it into some youth hostel or bingo hall.

Chorus of agreement and dissent. Irene Travis flicks her cigarette and I can't help wishing I'd bought some myself. Carol attempts to explain the difference between Grade I and II listed buildings.

– So they can't knock it down, she finishes, but there are all these restrictions on what can be done.

– Just like the Old Hall, someone says.

– Which was left to rot, says George.

– Which is where we come in, Petra says decisively. She turns to Irene Travis. – I'm sure that what we all want to know next is what proposals have been put forward to the Planning Committee.

Irene Travis holds her gaze for a moment.

– Can I just say, she says, that as far as I know, no one has any plans to turn anything into a bingo hall.

– That was just an example, begins Les.

– I know it was, says Irene, rounding on him. – But the *implication* is that we at Planning would pass any kind of proposal without considering the nature of the building first. Now, that's a common misconception. So I thought we'd knock that one on the head right away.

Les looks as if he might say more, but Irene Travis stares him down.

– But that *is* the kind of thing that happens, Marie says, and a chorus of voices agrees with her.

– What about Barston's Mill?

– And the Mill Pond.

– And the old schoolhouse – first school in Broadstones that were.

Irene Travis's voice rises above them all.

– Excuse me, she says, I thought we were talking about the workhouse here. Not having some kind of free-for-all.

Then Councillor Norris stands. He is dressed in a beautiful suit, and his eyes are very clear and blue. He speaks in a soothing way.

– Now, I'm sure no one wants this meeting to get out of hand – Petra doesn't I'm sure . . . He smiles at Petra.

– I've known Petra for many years now, and I've always found her . . . relentless would not be too strong a word, in her pursuit of the public good. Which is why it's always a pleasure to be asked to speak at one of her meetings. Now if we can just get to the actual proposals . . .

He brings out papers and adjusts his glasses. Carol slips quietly back to her seat, and Nigel Scowcroft says to me, This should be worth hearing.

He has moved his chair up behind mine. When I glare at him he winks and nods towards the front. I turn away again, feeling mildly outraged.

The list of proposals is brief. There are plans to turn it into a conference centre, sheltered housing or small business units.

– What about a museum? Petra says, and George says that it's a bit high up for sheltered housing, you'd need a chair lift to get all the old folk up there.

Behind me Nigel Scowcroft chuckles.

– That's George, he says. – You'll not put one over on him.

This is too much.

– Excuse me, I say, in the tone that Jamal used to say would freeze curry, but he only cackles again and rubs his long fingers. Ignore him, I think, and begin to wonder about going home.

Petra says that there have been four attempts now to get a museum or a heritage centre going, and the Old Hall would have been the perfect place.

– No one wanted it after the murder, someone puts in.

Nellie Flitch ran down that hallway shrieking like a steam engine, my mother's voice says in my mind.

– I had heard, George says, that Boyd had put in a proposal to turn it into private housing.

– Not that I know of, says Councillor Norris.

– Well, that's what they were saying at the Bull's Head, says George. There is laughter and Councillor Norris laughs the most merrily of all.

– As far as I know, he says, the Bull's Head is not the centre of planning for Broadstones.

– Yes, but, Larry, Petra says, what about plans for a museum? You know the one we have is tiny and inadequate, and I would have thought that with the expansion of tourism in the area it would be a real priority.

Councillor Norris is very reassuring on this point. The council are well aware of the need for a heritage centre, he says, and they are looking favourably on plans to create one. He doesn't know whether or not the workhouse will be the favoured site in the end, but he himself would give that particular proposal his full support. And the fact that it is a listed building makes any other kind of conversion unlikely.

– Then there's the trees, says Les.

– Yes?

– Well, it should be possible to get some kind of preservation order on them. After all, if Boyd does get the tender they'd be the first to go.

– It wouldn't be the first time, says George, and everyone agrees.

Boyd had built houses on a tip.

He'd had permission to build twenty bungalows up Stoneswood Clough and in no time at all thirty-odd three-storey houses had gone up.

Ponds had disappeared overnight.

He was dumping, quite illegally, at Brun Hill.

I sit back as the clamour increases. I've heard it all before. These are old battles, fought endlessly and endlessly lost. Yet another reason for leaving the area. At least in the centre of London hardly any more damage can be done.

I feel a comforting detachment. These are people who next week might be campaigning to have gypsies moved from Hollin Knoll, or bad council tenants relocated on to a little estate of their own, miles away from anywhere on the open moor. Petra just wants to be Lady of the Manor. But why is Paul so interested?

Irene Travis stubs out her cigarette.

– It seems to me this meeting's getting out of hand, she says to Petra. – And forgive me if I'm wrong, but I thought we'd been asked here to clear the air. Not to be put in the stocks and have mud slung at us.

Petra starts to protest, but George says, No one's slinging mud. All we're saying is, when Boyd gets his hands on a place nothing's sacred.

– George won't let them off the hook, says Nigel. – He was a conscientious objector in the war.

I shake my head, suddenly feeling the urge to laugh.

– It's easy enough, Irene Travis is saying, to paint us as the enemy. But we've got the Department of the Environment on our backs. Ten thousand houses have to be built in this borough alone – they have to go somewhere. And then you've got builders like Boyd – more than willing to make a nuisance of themselves until they get their own way. That site where he built the plastics firm – he was on to the council for years about that and he turned the whole place into a dump and an eyesore until he got what he wanted. I reported him, didn't I? she demands, turning on Councillor Norris, who says that she did, indeed, and that he had supported her.

– People are too handy at throwing blame around, she says.

– But this is beside the point, says Councillor Norris, and Petra loudly agrees.

– We do have several other items on the agenda, she says, and Marie says, Yes. She has mainly come about traffic on the school road, and if they weren't going to get round to it this meeting she could leave now and save herself some babysitting money, and the woman next to her with the mousy perm says, Traffic *and* parking.

Petra raps her stick on the floor. – I think we'd better move on, she says, but George says, But we haven't established anything yet.

– What do you mean, George? says Petra, and George stands up.

– Well, I'd like to know, for the record, exactly what Councillor Norris's position *is*, he says. – I'd like to hear him say, in plain English, *exactly* where he stands with regard to the workhouse.

He sits down again, and behind me Nigel snickers.

– Like a dog with a bone, he says.

Councillor Norris's pale eyes become even more limpid and clear. He had *thought*, he says, that he had already clarified his position. But just to dispel any residual confusion – he would certainly oppose any plans that involved fundamentally altering the nature of the building. He is very aware of the strength of feeling in the borough and he would support his residents as he always had. He himself feels that to lose such an important feature of Broadstones' heritage would set an unfortunate precedent, and he would voice his objections most strongly should such a move be contemplated.

– There you are, George, says Petra, sounding gratified. – *Now* can we move on?

There is another outbreak of grievances about the council tax, the bus service, the nursery. I stop listening. This might be the time to leave. They will go on all night, I can tell, batting the same points backwards and forwards. I shift forward in my chair, aware all the time of Nigel Scowcroft's eyes watching me intently; he has not stopped watching me the whole time. The next time Mary Brennan goes by collecting cups I whisper to her that I will have to go.

– Oh – oh dear, says Mary, what a pity. You won't hear the next speaker. And there's a cake.

I assure her that it doesn't matter, and follow her through to the kitchen. Mary apologizes all the time in a distracted kind of way.

– These things tend to get a bit out of hand – we're all very grateful – thank you very much indeed for coming – I haven't seen you at these meetings before?

– No, I say, and I end up telling her that I am renting, temporarily, up at Hurst's cottages.

Oh, says Mary, and stops what she's doing. – Well, now – I think we've got petition forms somewhere . . .

– I don't think –

– We're *desperate* for someone to do that end of Shaw Road, she says, her eyes settling on me suddenly with surprising focus. – There's not that many – just three or four sheets.

She ruffles through the papers on the kitchen table, while I try to explain that I'm not sure how long I'll be here.

– Oh. Oh, well – I'll just give you these few anyway, shall I? Then if you do get a chance – You just have to knock on the doors and ask people if they feel concerned –

As if, I think.

– You'd be surprised how many people feel the same way. And then just pop them back through my door. Or post them if you like.

I'm about to tell her that I certainly have no intention of collecting signatures when there is a crash from the lounge.

– Oh *dear*, says Mary Brennan, and Les's voice says, It's all right, Mary – nothing broken.

And I leave while the going is good, clutching the sheets Mary has thrust at me.

Maybe I should give them to Paul.

Outside, in the moist air, I begin to feel better. I'm not up to gatherings yet, I think. It was a mistake to go and remind myself of that world in which Broadstones is the centre of the known universe, and other places, London, England, Europe, peripheral. I walk away from it as briskly as I can.

Of course, what I should have asked, I realize, is where the bus stop is now. All the underbelly of the road has been unearthed in deep grooves strung with orange ribbon and winking orange lights. The road itself is still, almost unnaturally quiet. Trees on the far side stretch their branches silently, and behind them the great hill rises, a massive darkness. Everything is still, but with a kind of passion inside that I haven't noticed in the daytime, the passion of growing things, leaves and shoots pushing from the tips of trees, grass and leaves sprouting quietly from walls. Even the roadworks are generative in their own way, I suppose, if only of chaos. As I walk past the dirt piled high on either side of the road I can almost imagine prisoners-of-war emerging from the depths of the earthworks, wielding shovels, covered in clay, into an unrecognizable world.

I know where I got off the bus, but there is no corresponding stop on the other side of the road. I can't face going back to Mary's house, however, so I carry on following the water board signs. Sooner or later I will arrive at the headquarters of the water board itself.

Time unwinds itself on long spools as I follow the road. I have always been walking along it, I always will be. And however far I walk I will never get any nearer to the stop.

How much further, Mam?

Stop dawdling.

If only I'd brought the car.

Suddenly I know what I'm doing here, what has driven me to the meeting, to Broadstones, what is driving me along this road right now.

My mother, Susan.

I stand still for a moment, between tunnelling and the wall.

I never knew before that each death is a journey.

I put out a hand to the wall and feel the reassuring roughness of stone. All the unfinished business between myself and my mother seems to descend around me like rubble.

After a moment I carry on walking. But now my mother's presence is there, walking ahead of me as she invariably did when I was small.

Finally I see the small temporary stop, and stand by it, staring into the space where the bus should be. My mother's presence is all around me like a shroud. I feel very young, very vulnerable. All right, Mother, I think to her, I'm here, all right?

Unsurprisingly, nothing happens. I stand there, remembering what it was to be young. But what I mainly remember is being impatient for time to pass, waiting for Christmas, waiting for birthdays, waiting to grow up and leave. These days, especially since my mother died, all I want is to slow it down. Days in London rattle past like pictures on a fruit machine, too many things to do. That's why I'm here, in Broadstones, in a little vacuum of my own, trying to turn time around. Perhaps I should be grateful to the transport authority for taking the buses away, creating this oasis of time.

The sky is boundlessly clear with a slice of moon. I am actually cold, stepping backwards and forwards to warm my feet, gazing upwards at the first faint stars. Because the sky is still pale it's not easy to see them, but surely that's one, near the moon.

– Jupiter, says a voice in my ear.

I whip round, clutching my chest. It's Nigel Scowcroft, grinning like a cheese.

– Are you following me? I say in a rage. It's one thing being importuned at a meeting, but quite another being followed to a bus stop. I glance quickly along the street but there is no one I can run to for help.

Nigel seems genuinely surprised. He steps backwards with a curious, lolloping motion, almost dancing.

– No, no, he says, waving his hands. – I've just come for the bus.

I suppose this is possible, but I'm still wary. I look away from him, slipping my hands into the sleeves of my jumper, intensely aware of him all the time. *This isn't London*, I tell myself.

– What did you think of the meeting? Nigel says, and unable just to ignore him I say, Have you been before?

– Oh, yes, many times. There's always something on.

He talks as if it's a show.

– But do they get anywhere?

– Oh, no, he says at once. – There's nothing you can do. I'm about to ask him why he goes, then, but he says, Builders like Boyd, and the heads of the council, they're all in the same club.

– What club?

– You know, he says, you scratch my back and I'll scratch yours.

– You mean, like the Freemasons?

– Something like that.

I'm interested now, in spite of myself.

– What's this club called? I say, but he only stares at me cannily. I can't decide whether he's retarded or very wise. And I don't want to play any games.

I turn away from him and he says, More things like that go on than we ever know about.

Oh, conspiracy theory, I think. I can't be bothered with that one. So I ignore him after all, and then he says, If you look, there's almost a kind of halo around it. Almost.

Reluctantly I look where he's pointing, which is back to the star. I can hardly see it, faint and winking above a roof, never mind the halo. Glasses, I think, discouraged. My eyes are going. Nigel draws closer.

– It's an amazing thing, he says, in hushed tones, that round that planet right now dozens of moons are whizzing about, some of them not much bigger than a football pitch.

It certainly is amazing if you think about it, but I don't want to think about it. I blow my nose and stare harder into the space where the bus should be. Perhaps there isn't a bus, I think, and have terrible visions of standing there all night with Nigel.

– Jupiter has the fastest moons in the solar system, Nigel says, apparently unconcerned about the bus. – How fast do you think the fastest one goes?

– Is this a test? I say, and Nigel grins all over his withered face.

– Go on, he says, guess.

Go away, I tell him in my mind.

– Remember that Jupiter is over a thousand times bigger than the Earth, he says, and he gazes at me expectantly. I sigh.

– The fastest one, he says, is called Metis, and it does the whole orbit in .29 of a day.

His hand shoots past my face.

Vrrrmm! he says. – Like that. Only faster.

I step back, glaring. – Look out, I say, but Nigel goes on undeterred. Nothing will ever deter him, I can see that.

– *And*, he says, Jupiter also has the slowest moon in the solar system. Sinope. Orbital period 758 days. Over *two years*.

There is triumph in his voice as if he's arranged it that way himself. I crane my neck as if that might make the bus appear sooner. Perhaps it knows Nigel is waiting for it.

– Those two moons are up there now, Nigel says, both going round the same planet at those different times, fast and slow. And he waves his arms round simultaneously, fast and slow.

– I like astronomy, he says unnecessarily. – I mean, when you think how far it is to the sun, ninety-three million miles, and then think that all the atoms in your body, drawn to scale, are further apart than that . . .

I have a brief image of my body strung out across the universe.

– Blows your mind, doesn't it? he says, watching me solemnly.

I press the tips of my fingers to my forehead.

– Where *is* this bus? I burst out suddenly.

– It's here now, says Nigel, and miraculously here it is, an orange blur rounding the corner. Relief gives me a new burst of energy. I wave strenuously at the driver in case he doesn't stop. Nigel presses on closely behind me. I wonder if it would be too obvious to sit down next to one of the three passengers, but at the last minute sit instead in the middle of a double seat, and to my relief Nigel walks past.

I sink back into the seat. Thoughts of mass and time and gravity and secret societies and Henry Hawkyard and my mother whir in my head. I am suddenly unutterably tired. Sections of road flare in the sweep of headlamps, glittering tarmac, a fountain of fuchsia. Several places behind me Nigel Scowcroft hums noisily to himself, unaware of people looking round. Happily, he gets off first.

I am almost too tired to walk up the path to the cottages, open the door, make my way to bed without food. Not only tired but aching, I let my head sink into the pillow. I can still see a single star above the wooden frame that divides the window in two. It shines restlessly, flickering in the bowl of sky.

Jupiter, I think, and I imagine all those moons whizzing round or floating slowly, not borne down by the mass of information that weights the Earth. As my thoughts curve into sleep I feel that I would like to be free of everything I know. I would like my mind to be round and spacious, like the sky.

CHAPTER II

Martha

The whole world comes into a bookshop, rich and poor. And he stays open all hours so as to let the whole world in.

Poor people come in before work starts and after it ends, ruffling through the penny books, Tom Hickathrift, Goody Two Shoes, and the dearer ones, Ruskin, Shelley, with their raw, dirty hands. Children come in with rags round their feet, pus leaking from both ears and you have to watch for them pinching. It makes you think – who takes care of them, really? It makes me think about that workhouse van, hauling its cargo up that hill.

There's Gerry the workman who likes a good murder, and Miss Levette who wears a feathered bonnet and pretends she isn't poor, and laughs a laugh like peas rattling in a tin whenever he's there and will only read romance, long in the tooth though she is.

Then there's the rich folk. Alderman Patrice who's writing a history of the city – very long it is, so he has to keep calling in. And Mrs Wrentham, a handsome besom who'll only talk to Charles.

– Oh, yes, isn't that a Hallsby original? or, Canon Tilden provided the definitive commentary, I believe. To say such things, and to have him hear her, that gives a point to her day.

Some days it seems like the whole world's reading, hungry for words. I read too when I get a chance, Mrs Gaskell, or one of these 'New Woman' novels that make you burn and wish for different things, but mostly I don't get a chance. There's always something to do, dawn till dusk.

One day he comes running down the stairs with his face all livid so I fear something bad's gone wrong, but he catches hold of me and swings me round. Turns out he's had a case of books from Germany, Goethe, Schenk, Novalis and such, *and* at the *same time*, a letter's arrived from the Earl of Stamford, asking after those very books.

Between him stuttering and falling over his words I can hardly tell what he's saying. But he's supposed to go to Shude Hill this morning, for a copy of Newman's *Sermons* and the *Apologia*, only he can't leave the shop in case a representative of the Earl calls by.

– Anyway, he says, some men might be calling in later.

– What men? say I, very sharp and sudden, but he only goes vague like always, and mutters something about friends of his uncle's, and what can I say to that?

– I'll go, I say.

I like going out, even when it rains. I always walk, even when Charles gives me money for the tram. Who wants to rattle about in a bone-shaking carriage? And the road to Shude Hill's only at the far side of Collyhurst. Anyway, I miss walking. Miles and miles over the moors I've walked – what's a short walk down a long street to me?

I can see Charles thinking, trying to think. But if it comes to who I'll show him up to least, Earl of Stamford or Bill Travers of Shude Hill, there's no contest. So while he's thinking I nip and get my coat.

It's the time when a little spring arrives midwinter. The air's mild and there's a watery sun on the pavement. It lifts my heart to be out walking, even in these smoky streets, and the further I go the further it rises, till I think it might fly off like a bird.

Past navvies digging the road, past hoardings full of adverts, for Beecham's Powders and Wright's Coal Tar Soap, past railings where weeds are beginning to bud, and finally to the great warehouses that flank the city road, one after another, all the way in.

Shude Hill's swarming. Bookstalls, bric-à-brac, fish and oyster traffic in the little alleys by the Fishing Tackle House. So many people, coming and going! Like atoms in that New Science lecture Charles took me to at the Mechanics Hall – winking in and out of time and space. I can hardly get forward for people pressing and pushing, Excuse me – I'm sorry – sorry – I'm sorry.

And so many of them Jews! With their funny ways of dressing and speaking. Never do business with a Jew, Father said, for you'd never win. But he lost anyway, much he knew. They live here same as us, but not the same; in their own world and their own time too, seemingly, one world within another, rubbing up against it but never fully mingling. That's what strikes me about the city, that it's home to everyone and no one. Everybody lives here, but nobody's home.

When I first came here it was a shock. I knew the world was big out on Broadstone Moor, but I never knew there were so many people in it. When I got off my first tram I wanted to run off like a scalded cat. Now I'm used to it but it's still too much. Here a woman pulling two children along, you'll give me a headache, you will, there a bustle of pigeons rising before the wheels of a carriage, and a man pasting up posters for the Manchester Philharmonic right under my nose.

I can't find Bill Travers's stall for looking. And when I do find it I realize I've walked by it twice already, and there is Bill Travers, but as he's talking to another stallholder I can't go up. I busy myself looking through the items on his stall, which are mainly cheap reprints, and a few local pamphlets.

Then he sees me.

– Ho there, he calls, and comes over with his arms spread right out wide as though he'd take me in them if he could, but I step back sharpish and he drops them.

– This is a pleasant change, says he, and he looks at me in that way he has, very like a hawk.

– Mr Wrigley couldn't come, I say, speaking carefully and proper.
– He has an appointment. With the Earl of Stamford, I say, thinking, Put that in your pipe and smoke it.

– Has he now? cries Bill. – Well, well. Cause for celebration.

Especially since it means my humble stall being graced by your pretty face.

I feel my back straighten like a poker.

– He said you would have some books for him, I say, very prim. – Newman –

– Indeed, booms Bill, for all the world to hear. – The *Sermons* – and the *Apologia* – he says it funny –

– *And* – *The Dream of Gerontius*. Now then. And he reaches down and brings out a handsome, bound volume from behind his stall.

– Oh – but Ch – Mr Wrigley only sent money for the books he ordered, says I, nearly slipping up.

– Ah, but I'm sure he'll be well pleased when you take him this little treasure back as well. A first edition, no less.

Now I'm trapped, sure I'll do the wrong thing. And Bill Travers looking at me in that pressing way, and I feel about ten years old.

– Take it anyway, says Bill, but I don't know if he's being cunning or kind.

– I'm sure I'm well enough acquainted with Mr Wrigley, booms Bill, then he drops his voice.

– I'll put it on account, he says. – If he doesn't want it he's only to let me know. I take the volume, sure I can feel him tugging it back playfully before handing it over.

– I thank you, Mr Travers, I say, the way Charles has taught me. – I'm sure Mr Wrigley will communicate with you soon.

And he bows, all mockery and smiles, and the relief's hot in my face as I turn to go.

It would be all right without people, I think, stepping this way and that. It would all be fine. People show you up and hold you up and you can't get on for thinking.

But now at least I'm free to walk a little, past the black pinnacles of the cathedral, and the bulging mass of the Exchange, dodging the traffic, the endless stream of carriages advertising Bovril, or Seymour and Mead Tea, or Sunlight Soap. When I first came here I thought it meant they must carry Bovril or soap.

Why does a woman look old sooner than a man? it says on the side of one carriage; and Woodrow's, Soap Makers to the Queen, on the other.

Past shop windows where there are coloured lozenges in bottles, and cakes and sweetmeats are piled in shining heaps, like fruit and vegetables, only with turrets of whipped cream. I buy myself a little cake with the money Charles gave me for the tram, and eat it as I go, sucking my fingers, for once never thinking of him. When I look up I'm struck dizzy, one business piled on top of another, all the way to the sky. Moss & Son, Tailors, with Pioneer Insurance on top, Patty & Son, Watchmakers on top of them, Barnsley Bobbin-makers next and, at the very top, Sykes' Writing Academy. All them workplaces, and all the people who work in them whirring and buzzing like so many insects. It's hard to believe there are so many different kinds of work (all one work, Charles says, the work of commerce). And one day soon we might have a shop in the city, and I might have a straw boater instead of this old, crushed bonnet. For there are plenty of rich folk in the city, ladies in velvet and fur, and behind them, in doorways, poor people holding out hands. The rich people hold their hands out too, Charles says, only not on the street.

Everyone's going somewhere, or seems to be, one omnibus after another, packed full of people riding by, then a man on a bike, stirring the air. Across the main highway the flower stalls are out, and the first primroses and snowdrops are for sale in glass booths, with great branches of pussy-willow besides. Seeing them makes me think so sharply of the moor I can almost taste the sorrel in my mouth.

And there's a little girl by the corner, next to the snowdrops, with bright button eyes and very bright boots, and her mother's calling, Emma, Emma, hurry up, do, and with a trailing look behind at me the little girl catches up. Then there's a woman in a fantastical green bonnet, pushing a perambulator, and another selling pegs, and a smart man with a cane walking towards the great banks and insurance firms, and I feel lifted up by the commotion, like that night on the moor, with all the stars, when I knew that nothing really mattered. Sun lights up the hair of a raggedy little girl picking pennies from a grid, but when I look again she isn't pretty, too many sores on a pale, peaked face.

All round me buildings are being repaired or cleaned. Scaffolding up Yates' Wine Lodge reaches up to a cold blue sky, and suddenly I know it will always be so, the coming and going, the building and mending and tearing down. But beyond it, beyond the cold new shafts of sunlight, there is stillness, for what makes time move but the activities of men beneath the great, unhurried sky?

By now the books are heavy in my arms and I can feel the strain right down my back. And I'm still hungry, but it's time to go. Past the boy in the peaked cap pushing a steaming stall and shouting, Blood puddings! till my mouth waters, past the crowd gathered round two women who are calling for votes at the corner of Shude Hill, back to the Rochdale Road.

The road worsens as I go, litter and sputum and pools of yellow water in cracks in the pavement. And suddenly it seems a long way home, and I get to thinking about the two little girls, one with bright shoes and the other with sores, and how nothing accounts for the mystery of it. And how the one with sores might yet be loved, and the other not, and that's the bigger mystery, I think, and tears stand like soldiers in my eyes, ready to fall, for I can't help thinking of the child that me and Charles won't ever have. And so I go on, sorry for myself, and the weight of going back lands on me like a fall of snow. But then it comes to me that there is love in the world, that of all the thousands of people I've just seen, not one thousandth of the folk there are, there's not one of them but loves. And this cheers me up. For love's invisible, but it *is*, and everyone loves someone in his or her own way, though it might not be who they ought to love. I've loved. First my mother, as a baby, then Mill. And Mill loves all her children, especially the new one, Robert Arnold, just born. And even Anne loves Albert in her way. If you think of all the people who have ever lived, who are living now, and what a powerful amount of love has ever been, the world should be like a great flaming ball with it, burning and turning. Yet it's the misery that's more obvious, I think, stepping back to avoid having my skirts spattered all over by a passing bike. Still, love does its work and is passed on, like a family likeness, a handprint on the heart. For a mother loves a baby and that child loves in turn. And even those who've never been loved manage somehow, which is the real mystery, it seems to me. But I have been loved, I think, turning the corner on to Francisco Street. It's just that the way things are it's hard to pass it on. Yet sometimes I look at Charles's face and think, We're just two people caught in a storm, and if we could reach out to one another we'd be home.

Thinking this way warms my heart, and I tell myself that Charles will be happy too, first the Earl calling, now this unexpected extra book. And I call out to him as I open the door.

But the shop's empty and so's the parlour.

– Charles, I call again.

Nothing.

Then I hear a low, strangled voice, Leave me for the love of God, and another voice besides.

All my happiness drains away from me like water. The palms of my hands are clammy, my mouth shrivelled up and dry. I put my hand on the stair rail to steady myself and stare upwards, at the blank darkness of the attic door.

CHAPTER 12

Louise

The library's deserted. It's almost closing time and only Carol remains, poring over a file full of old photographs. I edge round her, waiting to speak, but she is absorbed, sitting very still with a peculiar expression on her face as though trying to thread the past through the eye of her mind.

I've come to see Paul. But only to give back the petition forms Mary Brennan gave me. It would be ridiculous, even for me, to loiter round libraries with lustful intent. Or to get further involved in something as labyrinthine and hopeless as battles with planning departments.

When Carol looks up I smile.

– Hi, I say, is Paul in?

Carol doesn't smile.

– I think he may have gone, she says. – I'll just check.

Resisting the urge to say, Oh, no, or, It doesn't matter, or any of the other things customarily said in order to give the other person the impression that their time is really much more important than yours, I let her go.

First I study the shelves, which are carved into ornate shapes, fruit and birds. Then I study the carpet, which is plain, hardwearing. Finally, after she has been gone an unconscionable length of time, I turn to the photographs.

More sepia.

Children at the Old Methodist School, Swineshaw. Bell ringers at the Heights Church.

I flick through them. The faces could be those of my distant relatives, or people my mother knew. The youngest sister could be in there for all I know, in this photograph, in which crowds are pressing forward to watch the Whit Walks. The more I look the more it seems to me that the whole of my po-faced, doomed ancestral line might be gathered together in the leaves of this album, shaking a collective head at me, its errant member, the one who thought she'd got away.

All right, I say to them mentally. So I wanted colour and life, something other than poverty, illness, despair. Is that so unusual?

Look where it's got you, they seem to sigh.

Finally, with some relief, I come to a photograph not taken in Broadstones at all, but in the city centre. It has been taken from a height, as though from the window of a tall building. Foreshortened people speckle the pavements, only their hats seen full on. I can make out some of the lettering on the buildings. Moss & Son, Tailors, Pioneer Insurance. There is an omnibus, and a man on a bike, a woman pushing a pram. A little girl stands, detached from anyone, by the corner of a flower stall, and to the other side of the stall a young woman is considering the flowers. She is tall and thin, angled a little in uncertainty.

Everyone is busy, absorbed in their own lives, while some unseen person captures them. There is a horse-drawn carriage, and a man in a bowler hat stepping on to it, that moment taken out of his life for ever.

All those people are dead now, I think, and I have the kind of feeling I can get when thinking about stars, or atoms. All those people absorbed in their stories, as if they could never die.

– I'm afraid Paul left some time ago, Carol says, near my shoulder. – Can I take a message?

Hastily I replace the album. – It's all right, I say, barely smiling. – It doesn't matter. Then because she carries on looking at me questioningly, I say, I was at the meeting the other night. I heard you speak – it was very interesting.

Carol pinkens.

– I thought I made a mess of it, actually, she confides. – Public speaking's not really my thing.

– You were very good, I say, in my most reassuring tones. Then, in case she suspects she's being patronized, I add, It must be very difficult – sorting out all the material.

– *Hopeless*, she says, putting the photographs away. – Paul wants us to get a book together, and maybe some community drama, for the festival next year. But there's such a lot of stuff that's not even catalogued. And it all needs organizing into storylines. We need a few good plots.

– History isn't like that, I say, thinking, A mass of stories with no plot.

Carol shrugs her jacket on.

– I'm going to have to lock up now, she says.

Outside the light is pale and pearly, and for a moment I stand watching the people come and go. This street could be that other street, I think. An old lady passes with a shopping trolley, children gather into a gang at the corner. Transient people, I think, and it comes to me then that time doesn't really move at all, that old moments keep recycling themselves. As I walk away from the library towards the Bull's Head, where, in half an hour, I will be meeting Dan, where Frank's dialect evening will be taking place, everything stands out with great clarity, red flowers on a sill, the transparent sky. Starlings swerve towards a lamp-post, settle, rise again and settle on the next lamp-post along. All the way along the road they rise and settle in mysterious formation, fanning into a cloud as they rise, then settling into a thin line.

I follow the line of lamp-posts, the mysterious movements of the birds. Dreams are our lamps on rainy nights, I think, remembering the quote from somewhere, though it is not night, nor rainy, and I'm not sure I have any dreams left. I must have read the phrase once in some old novel. It often comes back to me, along with all the other debris that returns.

Traffic moves through roadworks like a giant earthworm and a dog scuttles swiftly between cars. A young couple passes, linking and looking down, his hair in dreadlocks, hers shaved. She has a cross tattooed on one cheek. My awareness of these things is piercing, as if I've lost all my protective layers. If it could become more piercing, if I could be like a colander through which light passes, maybe I could look into the yellow lights and blue shadows of shop doorways, and see people emerging from the past, one after another.

It's not simply that these things have changed, I think suddenly. It's that I lived here for years without knowing the place at all. My mother knew it like the lines on her face, but to me it was only a personal trial, an obstacle course. And it comes to me as I approach the pub that I would like to see the workhouse for myself. My steps quicken as though I'm being driven up the hill by the ghost of my mother, because I want to see the workhouse.

– What for? says Dan, when I tell him.

– I just do.

He peers doubtfully upwards. The Bulls' Head is about half-way up Blackshaw Edge, the workhouse is at the top, just over the crest of the hill.

– Don't tell me you've never been, he says.

– I never have.

– But why now?

– If you don't want to go, I say, sounding exactly like my mother, I'll go on my own.

And I set off. Somewhat to my surprise, he follows.

He has made some effort tonight, I can tell. Pale linen jacket, good shoes. I wonder how muddy the road is likely to get later on. And I remember him phoning me to check whether I really was going to the dialect evening; he sounded terse, self-conscious. I wonder about this now, five yards ahead of him, climbing the hill.

Dan mutters imprecations as he slips on a stone.

– Shall I get the car? he says.

– The walk'll do you good.

– Are you saying I need exercise?

I smile enigmatically, wait for him to catch up.

– How are things? I say to divert him.

Things are fine. He hasn't heard from either Sandra or the kids yet, but then he doesn't expect to, necessarily, before the end of the school holidays. Meanwhile he's gone back to work a couple of days a week.

While he's talking the road peters out to a track, though beneath the mud there are cobbles. Dan mutters under his breath again.

– What was that?

– I said, if I'd known I was going fell walking I might have brought boots.

I face him. Feel a spot of rain on my cheek that seems to come from an entirely clear sky.

– Well, look – you go back if you want to. I'll meet you in the pub in a bit.

– It's *dark*, he says, as though this is out of the question. Though in fact it's only twilight. The first lights have appeared among the hills, clustering in the valleys. This is the world they never knew, I think, those forgotten people. Chains of pylons, bracelets of lights, yet still beneath it all, that primitive bleakness.

I turn back to the path, tread carefully, fearful now for my own shoes (canvas flats), and soon, because this final part of the incline is the steepest, feel my lungs pumping and sucking away.

– It just shows you how inaccessible this place was, I say to Dan, who is too entirely out of breath to reply. – I mean – how did people get here?

Only those acquainted with the bleak country around the workhouse, which stands at the top of a long and weary hill, can judge what it must be like for little children to have to be sheltered there after tramping in such a district in winter.

That was written in 1841. Now, all these years later, I want to see the place that sheltered them. I want to see the trees they planted, the view they saw.

– Did you say you've been here before? I say, stopping for a moment for Dan's sake.

– Many times – we used to come up here sledging.

– It's a long way for sledging, I say, then after a moment, You'll know where it is, then.

– Isn't that it? Dan says, pointing to the tips of a black mass just above the crest. I hurry on, impatient now, and come finally to a large yet surprisingly unimpressive building in an advanced state of decay. It is surrounded by abandoned outbuildings. To one side of it there is a sign saying SITE FOR REDEVELOPMENT. It is still isolated, the views magnificent if your tastes incline to the bleak. If you were locked in up here, I think, you wouldn't even want to look out.

– Grim as a woman's face on washday, Dan says.

– You wouldn't buy a house here then, I say, if it was done up.

– Well, I don't know, says Dan. – It'd depend on what they did. And access.

– You wouldn't be put off, then, I say, thinking, Incarceration, epidemics, madness, suicide.

– Nah, says Dan. – Slap a bit of paint around, a few window-boxes. Throw in an oxygen mask and a four-wheel drive. Jacuzzis, he says, getting into the idea, *en suite* bathrooms, built-in televisions. You could probably make a swimming-pool out of the septic tank.

I leave him and look for the trees.

There they are, between barn and outbuildings, a bunch of straggly, wind-blasted pines. Beyond them, through the dimming light, I can make out the Elizabethan E shape of the central building that Carol talked about, the stone flagging and gabled ends. I step back, trying to get an impression of the whole thing, of what it tells me, but it tells me nothing, and I turn away again, feeling an inexplicable soreness of heart. I don't know what I wanted to see up here but it wasn't this. Evidence, maybe. Handprints all over the walls.

– Can we go back now? says Dan.

I can't think why not. The air is getting colder. And damp. As Dan sets off I catch up with him and take his arm. There is something comforting about Dan. Reassuringly solid. Nothing disturbs him too much. Even the disappearance of his wife and kids hasn't left him completely traumatized.

– So what's the big deal about the workhouse, then? he says.

I tell him about the Residents' Association. And Paul.

– Oh, *him*.

– Do you know him?

– Paul Prosser? Everyone knows him. Though he's only been here five minutes.

In fact, Paul has been here three or four years. Dan is not sure where he came from, but ever since he got to Broadstones he's been stirring things up with the council. He's always writing to the local paper, he had demonstrations organized when the train service was cut. Dan doesn't know why he hasn't gone into politics instead of library work.

– Perhaps he thinks he's more in touch with people this way, I suggest. – Keeping them informed.

Dan snorts.

– Librarians Against the Forces of Darkness, he says. – But where were all the librarians when Hitler came to power? Or Pol Pot.

– You don't like him, then.

– I hardly know him. He just seems like a bit of a poser, that's all. It's all a bit contrived if you ask me, all this Saving Broadstones crap. People who come into the area, he says, with sudden energy, not the ones born here, the comers-in – come looking for something it seems to me. And when they can't find it they feel threatened. Start stamping about a bit – making a noise.

Is that true? I wonder. What's Paul looking for? What am I? And what about all the people in the Residents' Association?

The first street-lamps appear as we approach the pub, blurred and magnified by moisture in the blue air. Light from them seems not so much to spread as to be absorbed, as if the damp air is like a giant blue cloth.

When we enter the pub all is light and noise. Dan goes straight to the bar. I blink round at the brasses, which wink back and glow, and feel a buzz in the flesh of my face from the change of temperature. More photographs have been hung at the bar: Market Street 1891, Rush Bearers at the Parish Church. I stand still, momentarily unnerved by the contrast between this and those abandoned buildings on the open moor.

Voices are chanting in the back room.

– Shall we go through? says Dan, handing me a drink.

> Owd Puddle keeps an alehouse ut back o' Don't's o' Ben's
> He keeps a feightin cock an twothri feightin hens.

Three of them, Frank in the middle, are chanting together. Others, mainly elderly, are laughing and clapping and urging them on. We take a seat at the back of the room. Then suddenly Frank is on the table, a diminutive figure with a surprising bass voice.

> Cum dahn yoa Haighsiders
> Cum dahn yoa Pulesiders
> Cum dahn, cum dahn
> Cum dahn yoa Farsiders
> Cum dahn yoa Narsiders
> Cum dahn, cum dahn
> Cum dahn yoa Binsiders
> Un ole yoa Deignyedders
> Cum dahn, cum dahn, cum dah-ah-ahn!

That's the calling song from the Heights Church, Dan whispers, and indeed Frank's voice is ringing like a bell. I'm struck by the change in him, his voice, the way he stands, his face, all slipping into something older. I'm struck by all the waiting yellow faces, hungry for these leftovers from the past. It is like a circus of very elderly performers. Even so, as I listen, I can hear echoes of older voices in me, the voices I was so anxious to lose, my mother and her mother and her mother, the youngest sister too, I suppose. My great-great-aunt.

Frank's stance and expression change once more as he slips into a plaintive rhyme:

> When wur theau born owd rugged oak
> How many year hast seen?
> Theau'll never feel thi sap again
> Run thru thi boughs wi glee.
> And summer sun and winter rain
> Will come no more to thee.

I can't help thinking about the workhouse trees and why they were planted. They can't have been much use as either a windbreak or a screen.

When I glance at Dan's face he seems to be enjoying himself, but increasingly I feel as though I've wandered into a mausoleum full of photographs, brasses and this old dead language. I wonder why he's stayed here, in the place of his birth, and what he really thinks about the changes that are going on everywhere.

We clap enthusiastically as Frank climbs down, then again as he makes his way over.

– Thank you, thank you, that's very kind, he says. – I'm glad to see you've brought this lovely lady along to our humble gathering. A rose among thorns, he says to Dan.

I can't help smiling at this gallantry.

– You were very good, I tell him, and Dan says, It was grand, Frank, let me get you a drink.

Frank pulls up a chair.

– So how are you doing? he says, head on one side. – How's Broadstones treating you? And how's the family tree?

I have to tell him I'm no further on with the family tree.

– Is the recital over? I say, because people are dispersing.

– It might start up again later, says Frank. – We'll see how it goes.

– How's June? I say into a silence, and Frank's face deepens into melancholy, then brightens again as someone he knows goes by.

– As well as can be expected, he says. – She doesn't like me going out, though. It's all, Don't leave me, where are you going now – his face takes on the expression of a querulous old woman – We did have a nurse at one time, but I won't tell you what she called her, poor lady. She said she had a face like wezilled tripe. I told her, I said, June, you've no call to be personal, but one time she fairly spat and flew at her. Well, no one's going to take that, are they?

Frank sighs and his face is tragic.

– Fortunately my son and his wife are round tonight, taking care of her. Or I couldn't have come.

More relatives, I think.

– It keeps me going, you see, says Frank, and he tells me about the first time he knew June was ill, when he caught her pegging lettuce leaves on the line to dry. I can feel the burden of it, so acutely that it is hard to think of anything to say, but then fortunately Dan returns with the drinks.

– There's your friend and mine at the bar, he says, and beyond him, through the doorway, I glimpse Paul Prosser's face. Somehow this is the last place I expected to see him.

– He's the reason I've just been dragged all the way up Blackshaw Edge, Dan tells Frank. – To look at the old workhouse.

– Oh? says Frank.

– I just wanted to see it, I explain.

– It's a bad business, Frank says. – I remember when it was still in use.

– Load of fuss about nothing, if you ask me, says Dan. – What else are you going to do with an old workhouse – re-open it?

– Some people might think it's immoral, I say.

– That's very true, says Frank. – Everything with a bit of heritage round here's being snapped up by the money-men.

– And I can't see, I add, why anyone would want to live in a place where so much misery and suffering's gone on.

And Frank agrees with me again, but Dan says if that were true you wouldn't live anywhere.

– It's better than the new crap they keep putting up, he says.

– That's very true, says Frank, but, he says, with a rogue gleam, what do you think they'll call it when they're finished – Poverty and Hardship House?

– Damnation Row, says Dan, The Pits.

– The Abandon Hope All Ye Who Enter Here Mews.

– The Workhouse Mews, says Dan, raising a hand, a Highly Desirable Listed Building with its own mass grave.

In the general hilarity Paul comes into the room. He looks round, catches my eye, walks over. I can feel myself taking him in, checked shirt, jeans, stained canvas trainers.

– Paul, cries Dan genially, we were just discussing the workhouse.

Paul pulls up a seat, looks questioningly at me.

– We were just saying, Dan goes on, how much better it'll be when it's all done up.

I elbow Dan sharply but Paul ignores him. He is still looking at me with those black-olive eyes. How old are you? I want to say.

– Did you go to the meeting? he says.

– Don't tell me he's got you going to meetings, says Dan.

– I did, I say, but you didn't.

– Something came up, Paul says. – I had some research to do.

– Are you researching the workhouse? says Frank, looking immensely interested.

– Paul wants to get a book together, I tell Frank, of stories from all over Broadstones.

Dan snorts unattractively, but Frank says, Ah, well now, there's plenty of those.

– What I don't understand, says Dan, and there is a belligerent note in his voice, is all this sentimentality about the past. I mean – life goes on. You can't hold on to the bad old days for ever.

– Life does go on, Paul says, looking at Dan for the first time, but it goes on more in some people's interests than others, and there is a small crackle of hostility between them like an electric charge. Frank says that it's very true.

– No one listens to the people round here, he says, and what about those poor devils that lived and died up there? Whoever listened to them?

– For all you know, says Dan, they might quite like the idea of something nice being made out of all that misery.

– So you don't think profit comes into it, says Paul, making the odd million or so never entered Boyd's head?

Feeling that it is my role to intercept a row, I take the petition forms from my bag.

– Mary Brennan gave me these, I say, but I don't think I'll have the time.

– Petitions, Dan says. – When did petitions ever work?

– So what's your suggestion? says Paul.

– My *suggestion*, says Dan, is that you let the past lie. You can't help those people now.

Frank is reading the forms.

– I mean – what are you hoping'll come out of all this? says Dan, leaning forward.

Paul leans back.

– A long time ago, he says, the farmer at Hollin Clough took a boy and a girl from the workhouse to help out on the farm. Time went past but the children never seemed to get any older. But the farm was a bit remote, no one ever saw them in the village, and on the whole people kept themselves to themselves. So the facts only came out when a woman came all the way from Leicester, looking for the daughter she'd had to put in the workhouse when her husband died, until she got work. Turned out the farmer and his wife had been working the children to death, then going round to different workhouses replacing them with similar-looking children.

He looks round at us all.

– Don't you think that's a good story? he says. Don't you think that story should be told?

We stare at him a moment, and Frank says, And you want to put it into a book?

– A book, or maybe if we get enough stories, a series of plays focusing on the workhouse itself. We've already got the murder at the Old Hall.

– Oh, that's a good one, Frank agrees.

– If your tastes run to the ghoulish, says Dan. – I think you're wasting your time.

– We don't think so, says Paul, but, then, we don't drink at the same club as Boyd.

Ouch, I think, and Dan says, What do you mean by that? in a dangerous tone.

– I know someone in this row, Frank says, waving a petition form at us, who could tell you everything you'd need to know about the workhouse. Irma Stowe.

Paul and Frank look at me, but I'm still digesting the information about Dan drinking with Boyd.

– Do you think she'd talk to us? says Paul.

– Someone ought to, says Dan.

– Well, she's a queer old bird, Frank says, and Dan laughs. – Must be nearly ninety. But I know she used to look after an older lady who actually worked at the workhouse. She'd be well worth interviewing.

Paul and Frank look at me again.

– Well, I suppose I *could* go, I say doubtfully.

– Don't let them drag you in, Dan says. – You don't even live round here any more. And you're not from here are you? he says to Paul.

– What's that got to do with it?

– Well – all this interest in our heritage – I mean – why is that? Where *are* you from?

Paul mentions a small town near Huddersfield.

– But where are you *from*? says Dan, and I hold my breath but Paul smiles.

– My father was born there, he says. – My mother was from Bangladesh.

Paul's mother worked in a factory as a child of eight, just like the Victorian factory children. A sixteen-hour shift cleaning machines while they were still working – she lost three of her fingers that way.

– Now you see, Paul says. – In the Victorian period the rich made their money out of factory workers. And now we have the new rich moving into places like Broadstones, buying up property. And where did they make their money? Out of child labour in other parts of the world.

In the silence that follows, Paul's eyes become intent again.

– Do you think you might go to see this woman, he says, this Mrs Stowe?

What can I say?

– I'd still like to know what good you think it'll do, says Dan. – And who's funding this pageant idea.

Paul's eyes flicker once in his direction, then retreat.

– The Arts Board, he says, and we may apply to the Lottery.

– Not the council, then?

Paul looks wary.

– I'd have thought the council'd be the obvious place to start.

I can feel the tension between them again, though I'm not sure what Dan's point is.

– The council will contribute, says Paul.

– I would have thought so, says Dan innocently, it being a celebration of their borough and all. But don't the council get all their money from their Enterprise Development Agency, these days? He looks round at us all.

– If you've got a point, Paul says, make it.

– Well, says Dan, obviously enjoying himself, don't the Enterprise Agency do all their deals with property developers? Like Boyd? So your plans to save the great unwashed from the troughs of history, and reclaim the workhouse'll be funded more or less directly by the man whose only interest is in turning it into des res.

He puts his empty glass down on the table in triumph.

– Art buying next reaund? he says to Paul.

CHAPTER 13

Later, in Dan's car, I have the impression of not moving while street-lamps glide towards us. We have travelled home in almost total silence. I am of the opinion that he has shown himself up, he is of the opinion that I am now one of Tall Tosser's (as he calls him) lackeys, just because I have finally agreed to interview Mrs Stowe. All attempts at conversation have been brief.

– Dan, do you like living here?

– Mmph.

– You never thought about moving?

– Mm-mph.

– You must have seen a lot of changes.

– Don't start that again.

After a moment I say, So, where is this club, then, where you and Boyd drink?

Dan almost runs us into a tree.

– What is this? he demands. – Tosser's paranoia? I do not drink *with* Boyd. Sometimes he comes into the same club, that's all.

I let him calm down. Then I say, Which club is that? and I can hear him muttering under his breath.

– Vintners', all right? he says. – Vintners'. It's a club in town. Very select. Only followers of the Great Horned God are allowed in, to sacrifice virgins and goats on alternate Fridays.

– So long as I know, I say.

After this we travel in silence. Although I do feel a bit bad about dragging him up that hill and then subjecting him to Paul's moral crusade, so as he pulls up I say, Maybe we should have that picnic soon.

Dan still says nothing, but he inclines his head. I'm not going to beg.

– Give me a call, I say, closing the door.

Inside I make coffee, smoke a cigarette. Why am I still here? I ask myself. It seems to me that I've been creating reasons to delay going back, the Residents' Association, my family tree.

It's very quiet in the kitchen. My eyes are tired.

In London I didn't like being on my own at night. Towards the end of my time there I couldn't sleep unless all the lights were on.

I remain sitting at my kitchen table, looking at my fingers, which are interlocked.

I remember being in the kitchen of my flat, the last time Jamal cooked me a meal. The window was opaque in the electric light, reflecting a slanting image of the room, the image of Jamal unconsciously working. His elbow moved over a plate, a leaf from one of the begonias drifted quietly to a kitchen surface.

We are here, now, I remember thinking, and it seemed to me the most mysterious thing in the world. Out of all the times and places it was possible to be. When I looked at Jamal's face I had an image of it withering and loosening into age. I had seen him this way before, a few times since my mother's death; it made me want to be kind.

Now I sit with my eyes lowered to the kitchen table. If I raise them I will see an image of Jamal in the opaque window.

Slowly, steadily, I raise my eyes. I can only see myself.

In the morning there is a bad smell in the house. I wake up feeling physically oppressed. I check through the waste-bin, sniff the sink, nothing. There's a bad smell in the house and I can't open any of the windows. Finally I open the back door.

– Where are you off to now? Mary says at once. Meaning that I haven't talked to her for a while.

– Nowhere, I call up the stone steps. There's a bad smell in my kitchen.

– Drains, Mary says sepulchrally. – Henry's always saying he'll look into them, and he never does.

Mary seems more than usually truculent this morning. Perhaps she's feeling neglected. Cautiously I ascend the steps and sit on the fallen tree-trunk. I pluck at some creeping buttercup that is rapidly spreading from my garden to hers. Dilute sunshine is warm on the back of my neck, tiny spiders dance on the end of invisible threads. I tell Mary about the Residents' Association, and Mrs Stowe.

– *Her*, Mary says. – She's a funny bugger.

– Why?

– Won't speak to no one. Interview? That's a laugh.

I begin to feel that I've been set up.

– Do you know her personally? I ask.

– Irma Stowe? She used to do readings at Sunday school – looked after us littl'uns. Your mother, too, I should think. She was a right cow then as well.

I sigh quietly.

– Do you want some liver? Mary says. – You look pale.

– Thank you, no. I offer to shop for Mary while I'm out, she offers me bleach and disinfectant for the sink. Finally she stomps off in a mollified kind of way.

All morning I put off going to see Mrs Stowe – funny bugger/ queer old bird/right cow. I don't want to disturb her if she sleeps in the day, I tell myself. Or if she's having a bath. I pour Mary's bleach down the sink, sweep the floor in the kitchen and lounge, change the bed, write two brief letters I've been meaning to write since I got here. I tidy drawers, wash and trim the small, speckled cauliflower I bought from Joan and Cath, brew up, grate some cheese.

Mid-afternoon, when there is nothing in the world left to do, I set off down the road.

Mrs Stowe's doorbell is connected to an intercom, I notice, after all that worry about making her come to the door.

– Who is it? says a surprisingly strong, gravelly voice.

Feeling extremely foolish now I attempt to explain, about visiting the area, and the library project, and the workhouse.

– My name's Louise Kenworthy, I say. – You might have known my mother, Susan Kenworthy.

Pause. This is the longest conversation I've ever had with a small plastic door buzzer.

If she doesn't say anything soon, I think, I'm going away.

But the gravelly voice speaks again, telling me to come in, and I push the door, then when it doesn't move, put my shoulder to it until the stiffness gives way.

Inside there is darkness. Darkness and the old-woman smell of closed doors and windows, soiled clothing. Coming in from the bright afternoon it's like walking into an eclipse. I can't even tell where Mrs Stowe is until the voice says, Over here, by the back window.

Slowly I make out a clutter of objects in the room.

– I'm sorry to disturb you, I say, bumping into the leg of a chair. You must think it's strange, me calling in on you like this.

There is the soft thud of a stick against the arm of a small settee.

– Sit down, says the voice. I step over a jumble of something on the floor and sit on the edge of the settee, then wish I hadn't. Sunlight streams through a chink in the heavy curtains, and there is so much dust in it that I can hardly see Mrs Stowe.

Then she leans forward and we stare at one another without blinking. I hold her gaze for at least a minute in spite of the light, thinking what a large, craggy face it is, eyes like cracks in rock. Her legs stick out in front of her as though they don't belong. I can hear the crackle of her breathing. I'm not going to be the first to look away.

– Where are you staying? she says.

I explain about the cottages.

– You're all alone, then, she says, and for some reason her words chill me to the bone.

Suddenly she sits back. Released, I sit back also.

– I heard about your mother, she says. – Pass us that medicine, will you? She nods at a bureau where there is a bottle with a spoon inside a plastic bag. I get up, slowly.

All the room is flowered: flowered wallpaper, curtains, carpet, chairs. There are even framed prints of flowers, yet anything less resembling a flower than Mrs Stowe would be hard to conceive.

The bureau is in a kind of alcove and there is a tiny window above it with no curtains. Through it I can see the little park that is also visible from Frank's house, two swings and a see-saw, a rusty roundabout. It is empty now, one swing swaying lightly as if recently abandoned.

I hold out the medicine to Mrs Stowe, but she coughs into her handkerchief, a rich, bubbling sound, and doesn't take it. I hesitate a moment, then unscrew the lid. I feel as though I've wandered into the middle of a dream – my actions have the same quality of strangeness and familiarity: soon I will wake up and be back in my own bed, in my flat, in London.

Mrs Stowe opens her mouth for the medicine, and I have the sudden clear impression of the infant she must have been. But there is phlegm on her lips, and her tongue swells spongily in the pit of her mouth; it is spotted like a toad.

I try not to drip the medicine. Employing skills I didn't know I had, I scrape it off Mrs Stowe's chin and she licks the spoon, watching me all the time.

– Leave it there, she says, before I can ask what I should do with the spoon. I leave it and sit down, feeling suddenly more sure of myself, less discomposed.

– What's all this, then, she says, about the workhouse?

I tell Mrs Stowe about the Project, about Paul's plans to get a book together, or maybe a series of plays, as a kind of protest against the conversion of the workhouse into luxury homes. About Frank saying she would be a good person to talk to. By the time I've finished there's a smile like a crack on Mrs Stowe's face.

– Yes, she says, folk want to talk about the dead, but they won't talk to them.

I smile. I've had conversations like this before. My mother's sister, Aunt Katherine, used to be a regular at the local spiritualist church. She used to interrupt quite ordinary conversations by saying, over her shoulder, Wait a minute, don't be so impatient, I can hear you, all right, all right. Of course I was only a little girl when she died, and they used to shut her up whenever I came into the room, but I still knew what was going on.

So now I smile at Mrs Stowe until she turns her searching glance on me, then I say quickly, If there's anything you can tell us, we'd be grateful.

– Oh, there are things I could tell you, she says, but is it time? Is it time? she repeats, staring at the heavy curtains as if they might tell her. – Every story has its time, she says to me. I say nothing but glance down at the carpet, my feet, which do not belong in this strange room. Mary was right, I think. She won't talk to me. Mrs Stowe stares again at the curtains. In profile her face is even more craggy and impressive, but her chin shakes a little. I wait a long moment then say quietly, Frank Woodhouse said that you used to help out a lady who actually worked at the workhouse.

Mrs Stowe gazes hard at the chink in the curtains, as if willing them to part.

– Alice, she says eventually, in heavy tones, Alice Boardman. She was the teacher there.

– Really?

I remember Henry Hawkyard's letter, which seemed to suggest they were having difficulty finding a teacher for the children.

– Until they found out she had a child. Then they sacked her.

– Really? I whip out my notebook. It looks like the stories are coming.

– Of course it didn't start there, Mrs Stowe says. – It started, as far as these things ever *start*, with the Master of the Workhouse – Bernard Slater. A great bull of a man. And Henry Hawkyard, Clerk to the Guardians. It started with Emma Whately, who was only a child herself – fourteen or fifteen years old, and pregnant with the Master's child.

– When was this? I say, scribbling furiously.

– Eighteen seventy-one, says Mrs Stowe, very definitely.

– There's a display about Henry Hawkyard at the library –

– Alice reckoned he knew all along, says Mrs Stowe. He wouldn't have done anything if Alice'd've kept quiet about Emma. But Emma didn't keep quiet herself. She told everyone. Seems Slater'd promised her all sorts and she'd believed him. It was obvious enough whose child it was anyhow, with the men and women being separated off in the workhouse when they got there. But as time went on Emma got sick with the pregnancy and couldn't work. Others had to do her share, which went down well as you'd imagine. All Emma'd do was help Alice out with the littl'uns – reading to them and stuff. But she got more and more shiftless as time went on, and Alice had to do more and more on her own. Then one day Hawkyard comes by and asks if everything's in order, and Alice looks at him straight.

– It's not the classroom, says she, that's out of order.

– What do you mean? says he, and Alice looks at Emma.

– You'll not keep that hidden long, she says.

– Now Henry Hawkyard was mean as a flint and twice as hard. All vagrants slept in outhouses with one sheet apiece right through the winter while he was there. But even he had to mind the Board. So he looks at Alice sharpish and says, Who's to know? But Alice had had enough. She said, Plenty will if I tell them. She should have known better, you could say. But she always did have a sharp tongue in her head, did Alice.

– Henry Hawkyard didn't say owt, but his lips disappeared. And soon after Alice gets a letter from the Board, saying that it had come to their attention that she'd had a child out of wedlock, and was no fit person, etc. And that they'd notify other Boards of her deception – that kind of thing. Anyhow she had to go.

I have stopped taking notes and am listening entranced. No wonder the Victorians wrote melodrama, I'm thinking. Mrs Stowe's breathing rasps in her chest. I wait for a moment to give her a chance to recover, then say, Where was her child?

– Castleton. With her mother. He was the reason she'd taken the job in the first place. Not many teachers'd work in the workhouse. In the end they had to send the kiddies to the local school. But Alice had a son to keep. She sent all her money to her mother, every month. I always wondered about it, though, Mrs Stowe muses, because she was a very religious woman, Alice Boardman. Not well educated for a teacher, like, but knew her Bible backwards.

Man that is born of a woman is of few days, and full of trouble.

He is chastened upon his bed and in the multitude of his bones with strong pain.

See if there be any sorrow like unto mine, which is done unto me, wherewith the Lord hath afflicted me and sent fire into my bones.

– She had arthritis, you see, Mrs Stowe says.

Her head has fallen at a crooked angle, and despite myself I feel a smooth fear at the change in her voice. My back stiffens and Mrs Stowe laughs.

– Don't tell me you never hear voices, she says.

Voices?

I manage a strained laugh of my own. Though, in fact, I do hear my mother's voice, increasingly since that night at the bus stop. It harries me around the kitchen, monitoring my domestic performance.

Chop it up properly, girl.

That's no way to make a sauce.

Call that a meal?

But voices in the schizophrenic sense, or in the sense of speaking in tongues, no. I shake my head. Definitely not. Mrs Stowe turns away.

– I hear them all the time, she says.

– Why did Hawkyard stand by Slater? I say, trying to make sense of my notes and steer the conversation on to less treacherous ground. – And – couldn't Alice have appealed to the Board?

– They were thick as thieves, Mrs Stowe says, with a violent gesture. – Partners in crime. Not above adding floor sweepings to flour and serving sour milk. As long as they ran a tight ship, as they called it, plenty of profit, no one asked any questions. As for the Board, Mrs Stowe says more calmly, who'd've listened to Alice? No, she says, shaking her head, they were all in the same club.

Here we are again – Clubland. I interrupt Mrs Stowe as she is about to speak again.

– What club?

– Oh, you know, Mrs Stowe says, drinking circles. You scratch my back and I'll scratch yours.

– You mean, like the Freemasons? I persist.

– Freemasons, Rotary, I couldn't tell you. But I do know this. There was a tight network going for the placing-out of children in apprenticeships – very tight. Very much who you knew and how well you knew them.

My scalp prickles. I don't want to think about networks like that, about that kind of power. We hold one another's gaze for a moment, then I say, So Alice had to go.

– Alice had to go, Mrs Stowe agrees, back to her mother in Castleton. And a hard time they had of it. Lost her mother that winter and her son the next. No one'd employ her you see. She took in laundry and mending, but even that was hard come by. It was a miracle she survived.

Mrs Stowe pauses and spits into her handkerchief, and for a moment the darkness of the story swells inside me, beyond knowing or comprehension.

– What about Emma? I say tentatively, preparing myself for the worst.

Mrs Stowe turns her glittering eyes to me.

– Ah, well, now, that's another story. That was the real scandal. Because Emma Whately died, you see, and then it all came out. Because one of the other girls, Sarah Brigg, was pregnant as well. And what happened to Emma must have put the fear of God in her, because she testified before the Board that before she died Emma said that Slater had given her a bottle of medicine to make the baby come before its time. The chaplain was at the birth and either Emma or Sarah told him, and him and Sarah went to the

Board together. That caused a rumpus. Slater was called before the Board, and he got witnesses to say that Emma's baby weren't his at all but one of the vagrants', and that Sarah Brigg went with everyone. But then a chemist came forward – Kaberry or Kewberry his name was, not from these parts. And he said that Slater had visited him one night saying that an inmate was in the family way, and that he, Slater, should not like the pregnancy to go on as people might talk. Especially on account of the extreme youth of the girl concerned. And the chemist, not liking the job, had sent him on his way. But Slater must have found another chemist. Because Emma was in her seventh month when she went into labour. And *she* died but the baby lived. So Slater's plans went awry, you might say.

– And he was dismissed. Though nothing was ever proved as such. Him and his wife were dismissed and were never heard of again.

Mrs Stowe coughs a long time into a handkerchief until I get quite worried and pass her the glass of water on the little table nearby. When she settles, breathing hard, I say, What about the baby?

Mrs Stowe can hardly speak for breathing. Eventually she says, Well. First the chaplain took it off, feared for its life. But he couldn't keep it. He had no wife and he was moving on. He made some attempt to get it fostered, I think. But times were hard and no one wanted an extra mouth. So back to the workhouse it went, once Slater was out of the way. And Hawkyard. He retired, though muck never stuck to him. And it just goes to show you how well he'd done out of his stint as Clerk, because he sold his own place and bought the Old Hall.

– He was murdered, though, I say.

Mrs Stowe nods.

– Couldn't have happened to a nicer chap, she says.

I look down at my notes again. They are scrappy and hurried. I only hope I can make sense of them later.

All the time I'm examining my notes I can feel Mrs Stowe's eyes watching me, which is off-putting. I feel I have to ask the right questions, not leave too many gaps. I don't particularly want to come back. Eventually I say, What about Alice?

– Some years later, says Mrs Stowe at once, as if waiting for that very question, Alice came back to Broadstones looking for work. She hung around the market, hoping for left-over food, and who should she get talking to but Nellie Flitch, Hawkyard's cook at the Old Hall. Nellie didn't know Alice from Adam, but she'd been looking for someone to work in the scullery. What Hawkyard said when he found out I don't know. Maybe it suited him to see her brought low. Or maybe he just wanted a maid. Anyhow, Nellie Flitch took her on and there she stayed. And sometimes, if they needed help, she'd do some cleaning at the workhouse for extra. That's how she came to see Emma's boy grow up. And be properly apprenticed. To a bookseller, Manchester way.

My mind is racing. I'm trying to remember what was said about the scullery maid in the passage about Henry Hawkyard's murder. 'The scullery maid was paralysed with fear' – was that it? 'Rendered motionless'?

– They never found out who did it, I say.

– No, says Mrs Stowe, with her glittering look, they never did. Alice was there that night right enough, but if she knew she weren't telling. One thing's certain, though – it weren't that man they charged with it. They had to let him go.

– And that's as much as I know, she says, and once again I hear the ruckle of her breathing.

I sit back on the flowered settee. I can see more clearly now in the darkened room. There are whorled shapes on the curtains that look like skulls, but are probably more flowers. One part of my mind is taken up with the darkness of the story, feeling acutely its horror and despair, but with another I'm thinking how perfect it is for Paul.

– It's a remarkable story, I say faintly, thinking, A real Victorian melodrama, and into my mind flash all the images I have ever had of the workhouse people, downturned heads, bent backs, elbows lifting and shifting in the rhythm of work, the crook of an eye glinting, a flurry of ashes in a blackened grate, and those wasted hands pressing seeds into the cold earth.

Mrs Stowe turns her impenetrable gaze towards me. – Do you happen to know, she says suddenly, if spiritualist church is still there?

Somehow nothing she says surprises me.

– I think so, I say. In fact, I know it is. More of a big house than a church, on the main road between Blackshaw and Harrop. Blackshaw and Harrop National Spiritualist Church, it says on a plaque outside. Established 1901.

– There used to be a medium there, Mrs Stowe says, called Edie May. I used to go after Alice died. I was never much for it, all this communicating with the Other Side, but I went anyway, just to see. I never got any messages, though. And them as did I weren't impressed by. Anyone here know a Jack? And Doris says keep your feet warm – that kind of thing. Funny reason to cross the Great Divide, if you ask me, just to tell someone to keep their feet warm.

I smile sympathetically. Mentally I'm preparing to leave, but Mrs Stowe goes on, She was a big woman, Edie May, with a big chin and a shilling on her head as we say round here – thought she was someone. Anyway, I got a bit sick of it all, and one night I think it showed. Because she came up to me and said, You're surrounded by spirits, young lady, but you won't let them in. Seeds falling on stony ground, she said. I didn't take any notice. In fact, that was the last time I went. I was a bit disgusted, like. But now, well, I know Edie May must be dead and gone long since. But sometimes I think I'd like to go again.

– Couldn't anyone take you? I say after a pause, but Mrs Stowe shakes her head.

– It's the stairs, she says, and the seating. I can't sit on benches. This is the only seat in the house I can sit on.

I lean forward a little, almost touching the legs that seem so cold and dead.

– What made you go after Alice died? I say, and Mrs Stowe looks at me for a long moment.

– She left me some money, you know, she says hoarsely. – Well, there was no one else. I was only a girl, but I used to fetch and carry for her, call in after school, or on my way to work. I wasn't expecting owt beyond the shilling she gave me, but she left me a tidy sum. Enough to put down on my first house, though I was only nineteen. And I was grateful. I never knew she had money, but I did know this – she never worked from the day Hawkyard got killed. And after she died, we were going through her things and I found something. It's in that bureau, there.

She nods at the bureau with the medicine on top, indicating that I should go to it.

– Second drawer down, she says, and draws deeply on her inhaler.

There is a little key in the drawer. I turn it.

– There's a box, says Mrs Stowe, to the left.

Indeed there is: a dark-coloured cardboard box, embossed with gold.

– Open it, she rasps.

Nothing surprises me in the atmosphere of this house. I open the box and inside there is a gold pocket watch, speckled with age.

– Look at the back, says Mrs Stowe.

On the back of the watch I can make out dim lettering. H.H., it says.

– Now does that look, Mrs Stowe says, her voice husky from the inhaler, like the kind of present a master of the house might give to a scullery maid?

I feel as though all the stories of Broadstones are unravelling before me. I can only stare at the watch, pass my thumb across its roughened surface. I am remembering the date of the murder, 1891. Emma's boy would have grown up by then.

– I hid that away, Mrs Stowe says, before anyone else found it. I didn't think Alice'd appreciate questions being asked.

– No, I say. I put the watch back in its box.

– Then I thought, Maybe there's something she'd like to tell me. Which is why I went to the church. But she never came.

– The dead are around us all the time, says Mrs Stowe. – That's

129

what Edie May said. But not Alice. Nor Henry, for that matter.

I step back to the settee, start gathering my notebook and pen.

– It's not as if they couldn't come if they wanted to, she says. – I've seen plenty of others. In the house. On the street. Sometimes you don't even know you're looking at them, says Mrs Stowe.

– Who? I say.

– The dead, she says. – They don't look any different from the rest of us.

I don't want to listen to this.

– You've been a great help, I say, picking my jacket up.

– Little Tom now, says Mrs Stowe, as if I haven't spoken, I see him on that playground with the other kids, broad as daylight.

She nods towards the tiny window.

– I used to wonder why the others weren't playing with him, then I realized they didn't know he was there.

I slip my jacket on.

– I'll tell them to let you know, shall I? I say. – How the Project's coming on?

– He knows I can see him, she says. – He even waves now. I don't think he ever had a playground when he was alive, so he likes them now. Makes sense, really, she says.

She is leaning forward again and the light from the window catches her eyes. If Mrs Stowe is mad, I think to myself, with a sudden qualm, or suffering from Alzheimer's, can I still use her story?

There is a look of great cunning on her face.

– You don't believe in it, do you?

I smile, shake my head.

– Yet there's a great many spirits round you, a great many. And I can see your mother plain as day.

My smile becomes still.

– She wants to speak to you but you won't listen.

– I'll have to go, I say.

– Yes, all right, she says, but evidently not to me. She raises a hand. – I'm telling her now.

This is definitely time to leave.

– She's saying, Mrs Stowe says to me, that the fall you had saved you from another kind of fall.

I feel a rush of blood to my face, a sensation like water where my bones used to be.

Mrs Stowe smiles indulgently.

– Nothing ever goes, she says. – You can tell that to whoever ends up at the workhouse once it's all done up. Tell them that from me.

I open my mouth to speak, then close it again. Mrs Stowe is still looking at me, malevolently, I think, with those glinty, malignant eyes. I feel that I might faint, or be ill. There is a torrent of voices in my head, but I can't speak. Abruptly I turn and fumble for the door.

– Tell them they're welcome to the story, Mrs Stowe calls after me.

Then I'm outside, astonished and dazzled by the sun, as if I've forgotten there is such a thing as sunlight. There is a great pressure in my chest. I stand still a moment, attempting to breathe, then set off along the road as if all the hounds of hell are following.

CHAPTER 14

Martha

Lately Martha had been ill. Charles had had to get a woman from the next street, Mrs Tetlow, to do the housework and press his clothes. He had done the cooking himself, feeding Martha the watery soup he made. She sat back on the pillows, opening her mouth for the spoon.

Mrs Tetlow talked all the time.

– There'll be a child on the way for sure, seven months married and white as a basin. I only hope you've more luck with yours than I had with mine – two fine sons both dead now – I left it too late to marry, far too late, past thirty, still to lose both . . .

She shook her head and Martha almost thought she would cry.

– Ah, but I wasn't a young thing like you – you could have twenty sons, eh? and she laughed instead, a short barking laugh, then clucked and tutted.

– But who's to say, eh? How long any of them'll live.'

She said these dark things with a cheerful smile, punctuating them with her short laughs, and not waiting for any reply. Once, Martha had lifted her head briefly from the pillows and said, There is no child, but Mrs Tetlow only clucked and tutted and said that she wasn't to fret, and the first was often the worst. So usually Martha pretended to be asleep when Mrs Tetlow came in, though she still had to endure the tutting and sighing and the short barking laughs she made as she moved about. She wondered if Mrs Tetlow was nursing the vicar also, and if that was why he had been ill so long. For Martha had thought she might go to the vicar. She needed to talk to him, to someone, about Charles. She had been waiting for a reason to go round and talk to him, but for weeks now there had been a series of different vicars. And some of the congregation said he might soon see that infinity he talked about, though he was not yet thirty.

So it was easier not to talk, to do nothing but sit propped up in bed, watching the brief sunlight flit across her hands. Aged, reddish hands they seemed, far older than Martha, and sometimes they would move involuntarily, as if they did not belong to her at all, from one square of the patchwork quilt to another, the fingers working constantly against the material, which was a habit she had had since childhood, of testing things by touch.

Millicent had made the patchwork quilt, and had given it to Martha the day she married. And recently she had sent Martha a prayer book for her birthday, as if she'd known somehow there was trouble. Charles had opened the package, and had left it with her when she had shown no interest. Later she had picked it up, examining it carefully, but there was no inscription, which was unusual for Millicent, who always wrote a special message. She had written recently, though, telling her about Robert Arnold. He had come a little early, and she was tired, but very well. That must be why she had forgotten to write in the prayer book. After a moment Martha had picked up a pen and written in it herself briefly, just the details of her birthday, 20 March 1904. Then she lay beneath the quilt, as if exhausted by her effort, and thought about visiting Millicent.

That was the thought she had come to, the night she had been taken ill, running along the bank of the river, nearer and nearer to the coloured waters.

I'll not go back.

I'll never go back.

The words sobbed in her chest.

She remembered from that night the wraith-like people beneath the bridge and, as she leaned over the muddy water, feeling the impulse in her flesh, in the cells of her flesh, to sink in, and let the waters close above her head. Then instead she had wandered up and down the bank in a distracted way, and it had come to her that she could go to Millicent's, she could go and help with the baby.

But still she wandered, for it meant going back to the shop to pack her bag and wait till morning, and she went on walking up and down in a troubled way, so that it was almost morning when she returned, and she was already ill.

But she could still go, Martha thought, plucking at the material of the quilt, and watching a sparrow peck at the window-frame, once, twice. She was getting much better. Any day now she would be strong enough to go.

For it was not the bargain she had entered into, she told herself with a shudder. She could not be obliged to stay.

The next evening Charles suggested that they take a walk. Martha leaned on him heavily, feeling the thinness of his arm through his worsted coat. If anything, he had redoubled his efforts in the shop since Martha had been ill.

There was a spring rain, but it seemed less to freshen the air than to release odours. Martha stepped over the soiled water collected in cracks in the pavement. There was a pigeon pecking at the muddied paper in the gutter. Martha remembered how, the first time she came to the shop, there had been a gathering of pigeons outside it, and she had felt the urge to run at them, and known she could not.

They passed the navvies, still working on pits in the road, and the posters on the Unitarian Chapel, begging the workers to give up drink. They passed the great yard with ropes strung across it, where the drunk and destitute could sleep, and suddenly a cluster of new leaves pushing their way through cracks at the base of the railings caused Martha a sense of homesickness so acute it brought a bitter saliva to her mouth. She could almost smell the sorrel on the brown moor, and taste the great open reaches of sky.

Martha couldn't help but wonder at this power of memory in her, so that her past life seemed more vivid than the present. Yet it was here, beneath her feet, beneath the paving, the same brown earth of the moor. All of Collyhurst was like a cracked and pitted skin stretched over it. In the same way, beneath the new Martha was the girl who ran over the moor with no shoes, speaking a wild, rough tongue. And it occurred to Martha that maybe everything was always eternally present, but visible differently, like the kaleido-scope Charles had bought to amuse her in her illness; the same elements in ever-changing patterns.

Other couples were out walking, and a boy on a bike rode past spattering mud, and men were gathering outside the Duke of Wellington. Collyhurst was always busy, crammed with people so you could hardly breathe. Yet once, Martha remembered, she had woken early, before Charles, and had slipped downstairs for the milk. And all of Collyhurst had been rimed with frost, the sky dark and pale and ruffled with pink, like the texture of rough wool. All of Collyhurst seemed to be sleeping, and for the first time Martha had felt the mystery of what went on behind the quiet doors and blank windows, and the mystery had a kind of beauty of its own.

Martha walked on, feeling through the soles of her shoes the craving of her feet for the earth they knew. They passed the poster on the side of the Duke of Wellington, on which there was a lady with coiled hair and a bottle of cod-liver oil, and then the notice on the empty warehouse:

Repent

For the Day of Judgment is at hand.

Prayer meeting led by Ebenezer Byrom, Thursday at 8 p.m.,

And Martha could almost hear the singing,

Sowing the seed by the daylight fair,
Sowing the seed in the noonday glare,

the way she had heard it many times walking past. And then, one time, she had persuaded Charles to go. For the vicar of St Malachi's showed no sign of returning, and Martha had heard that this preacher could heal with the laying on of hands. And she had wondered what that might feel like, imagining a flame like the top layer of her head being flayed, and she and Charles kneeling together, the tears streaming down.

So they had gone, and stood among the workers. Men and women with worn faces, or covered in greyish dust from the building sites, looking like ghosts in the yellow light, stood or sat on pallets and upturned crates.

The preacher was a large man with stained whiskers. He stood behind a makeshift table, and at first just talked to his audience, it was a kind of dialogue between him and them.

– You're all working men and women?

– Aye.

– All of you?

– Aye.

– You work hard for your living?

And so it went on, the preacher extracting from them the details of their lives like a confession, they lay in bed sometimes on Sundays, they went to the pub.

– Is that wrong? he demanded. – Is not your free time your own?

The murmurs of assent were less hearty by now. The preacher glared round at them all.

– You poor damned unbelievers, he roared, and everyone jumped. The effect was electric. Face working with emotion the preacher told them what they were really doing, day in, day out, digging themselves deeper and deeper into the Pit.

His eyes glared, his whiskers shook, his big hands clawed the air and clenched into fists.

Behind him singers sang,

> Rock of Ages cleft for me
> Let me hide myself in thee.

– Think of your last day, the preacher cried in agony. – When your dying eyes close for the last time – then fear will come on you like a storm and calamity as a whirlwind.

Martha hardly dared look at Charles, but when she did, she saw that he looked a little pale, but steady.

The preacher banged hard on the little table.

– Come forward, come forward, he roared.

Through all the singing his voice rose and fell, thundered and quivered.

– Come forward to salvation.

Martha felt very hot. Sweat ran down the back of her calico gown and she could hardly breathe. The preacher's eyes had fires in them, just like the Devil, she thought, and chills ran up and down her sweating spine.

The woman next to Martha wept quietly and people tottered to the front to be saved, while all around the singing and roaring surged like a storm. Martha was sure Charles would go up. She felt the need powerfully herself, to throw herself forward and make the voice stop.

But Charles remained quiet and restrained, keeping one hand on Martha's arm. As the meeting drew to a close, he guided her to a side door, and they left while no one was looking. And Martha's fingers shook so that she could hardly fasten her coat, but Charles only looked at her in his impenetrable way and said, Shall we go, then? and they walked quietly away from the warehouse, past the poster on the side of the Duke of Wellington, where the elegant lady with the coiled hair and long fingers lightly caressed a bottle of cod-liver oil.

Martha skidded on wet paper and Charles held her up. And she couldn't help wondering now, as she had wondered that night, how it was that Charles had remained so very calm, when at other times he would break into madness for no apparent reason. For there was St Malachi's, with its text above the door, that one time she had heard Charles chanting, all by himself in his attic room. *See the day is coming, burning like an oven, when all evildoers shall be stubble*. And in his hand he held matches, and on the table there were books, though when he saw Martha he cleared them hastily, and said, without turning round, I will be down in a minute, and she had asked him what he was doing, but he wouldn't say.

Then Martha had taken to praying herself, using the prayers from her book, because for all she knew they might be burned alive in their beds. And prayers came easily to her, connecting the language of the world she had known to that of this new, dark world. When she ran through a stock list, or cooked the evening meal, prayers fell continuously, quietly from her lips. In the mornings, even before the knocker-up tapped on the window, Martha woke already muttering prayers, and in the evening when the lamp-lighter came she could hear herself murmuring, Dear Lord, support us all the day long of this troublesome life, until the shadows lengthen and evening comes, the busy world is hushed, the fever of life is over and our work is done. Then Lord in thy mercy grant us safe lodging, holy rest and peace at the last.

They could see the lamp-lighter now, moving from one lamp to another along the Rochdale Road, and each lamp he came to guttered and sparked, then flared. Her memories were like that, Martha thought, rising and guttering to the point of extinction, then flaring again.

– Shall we go back now? Charles said, but Martha wanted to walk on as far as she could, though she was tired and had to concentrate fully on her walking and the way the street-lamps seemed to move with her, their light and the gleam in shop windows, in water along the street moving up and down, up and down with the slight, irregular motion of Martha's footsteps.

The night she had run to the river, the yellow lights and their reflections had run with her, jigging and jumbling and tumbling in her vision. That was the night she had returned from Shude Hill and, hearing voices in the attic, had ascended the stairs very quietly, fear running through her like water, and had pushed the door open a chink.

– Get out, get out, Charles shrieked, but not to her. When the violent beating of her heart receded she saw papers scattered on the floor, though she could not at first see what they contained.

– I will go, a strange voice said.

– Yes, yes, sobbed Charles, but then there was a noise as though he had flung himself on his knees.

– Don't leave me, he begged.

Martha raised the lamp she was carrying. Charles was huddled naked on the floor, fingers clawing at the papers. There was no one else at all in the room. Martha swayed backwards, as at a blow. Charles lifted his face, it was wet, with a slackened mouth, and at the same time what was on the papers came suddenly into focus. Drawings. Obscene drawings, not like the pictures in the *Anatomy.* Naked people with their limbs splayed. Women with animals, children with men.

Blood rushed and hummed in Martha's face. She didn't know how she got down the stairs without stumbling or crying out. She had run past her room and the door to the shop, fumbling with the catch to the outside door, then out, into the thick, cold air.

And she had thought about many things that night, about the time she had come upon him driving a paper-knife into the rosewood table, with an action like stabbing someone over and over.

– Stop it, Charles, she had begged, but he didn't stop. Martha was very frightened, then a small part of her went cold and still. When the fit was over she fetched a cloth and wiped the traces of blood from the table, then draped a cloth over it.

Then, weeks later, she found him working on the table with a fine pen, trying to cover the marks he'd made. She flinched at the sight of them but he was smiling.

– A little wax pen, he said, does just as well as any French polishing.

Martha didn't know what to say. She wished he would cover the table again with the cloth. Charles stood and went to her side.

– It doesn't matter, my love, he said.

Martha looked away.

– Do you think you're not worth more to me than one old table?

Martha stared at him. He started to say something else, but she flew to the other side of the room.

– You did it, she cried, you – I didn't do it.

Spittle flew from her mouth. When she looked at his eyes she knew that what they saw was alien to her, that there was nothing knowable in the world.

But then there were the others, the ones who dressed like circus freaks and stood about the shop, or asked to look at esoterica, which was kept in a special section, and Martha wished very much that Charles would not keep it at all. And Martha had sorted through the penny dreadfuls with numb, clumsy fingers so that she could watch them and watch them talking to Charles, the way he shrank before them; it was like watching a light being slowly extinguished. Martha worked on, and the flesh of her arms and hands grew cold, but her face burned. There was a feeling of pressure at the base of her skull and darkness settled at the periphery of her vision.

Suddenly she could bear it no longer, and ran at them, surprising herself.

– Eaut, she cried, in her old speech, pike off, eautcumblins –

One of them, a fat man, laughed in surprise with his fat pink tongue. Martha would have hit him, but Charles caught her flailing arms, and pushed her back with a look of horror on his face, whether at her actions or her words she couldn't say.

– Kibe at me, tha croot, yawnecked twitcher, she bawled, and Charles drove her out. Then for days he would hardly speak, it was as if he had retreated to some place far inside himself. And when she demanded to know who they were he said she was not to interfere, or take any notice of those men, they were nothing, business associates of his late uncle, they had helped his uncle and they were helping him, that was all.

– *How?* Martha wanted to know, but she got no further. And she had thought about all these things as she had paced the riverbank. Her prayers fell away from her and she felt that she was seeing and hearing fully for the first time. And when she finally returned, near morning, he was waiting for her anxiously, he had not been to bed. Damp was clinging to her, and shreds of grime from the streets, and he insisted on helping her out of her wet clothes, and drying her hair, and putting her to bed, and before he left he clasped both her hands in his and pressed them briefly to his forehead, but even in her exhaustion she felt a deep revulsion for his touch.

She felt it now, shuddering in the cold street so that Charles paused.

– We must go back, he said, and she let him guide her back the way they had come, conscious now of the harsh breathing that caught in her side. Then by the church Charles paused and Martha had to stop too. She became aware that he was looking at her in the way he had sometimes, as if a great pressure was building up. Martha looked sharply at him. She had learned to recognize by the changes in his face when the bad times came, the sunken, drawn-in look, even the texture of his skin seemed to coarsen, but he did not look like that now.

– There is something I need to tell you, he said.

Martha looked away from him with a pang of fear. The impression of his face stayed with her, yellow and old in the gaslight, that deep uncertainty there but not the madness.

– You do not know, he said, where I come from.

– No, said Martha, but not as if she wanted to know. She felt that he might be going to tell her everything, answer all the questions she had ever asked, yet suddenly she did not want to know.

He told her that he had been born in Broadstones workhouse.

Martha had the sudden impression of the wooden van rattling up the moor. But that wasn't Charles, she thought.

He told her that he had been fed and clothed there, given a kind of education, paraded before inspectors, the Guardians, and the good ladies of the Women's Institute. Then, when he was ten or eleven, he had been selected by Mr Wrigley, who needed a boy to apprentice to the trade of bookselling.

Charles stopped talking and a great silence grew between them. At length Martha said, Mr Wrigley – wasn't your uncle?

– My guardian.

Her father couldn't have known this, Martha thought. Then,

just as surely, she thought that he must have known, all the time.

– I was one of the lucky ones, Charles said. He told her that not every child survived apprenticeship. And he said more, terrible things about the workhouse, about being left in a room full of sick and dying children, and how, when you were let out from work, the cold air hurt your lungs, the white, pure light your eyes.

He said these things to her without emotion, but with a kind of painful, stupefied surprise, as if such things were hardly to be believed, even when you had lived them.

Martha thought about the way he touched her, as if fumbling with clay, and the way that sometimes he would put out a hand to her, not as if he wanted her, but as if he wanted someone to touch.

– What about them men? she cried suddenly. – Eautcumblins.

As she said it she realized suddenly that he would know that word, that all along he had known the speech he had told her to suppress, and that he must have been taught to suppress it too. He looked at her and she could see his throat constrict, as though swallowing all the words that would never be said between them.

Finally he said that they were helping him. They had helped his uncle and they were helping him, and there were debts to be paid. Debts to be paid, that was all.

– What debts? Martha said, but he wouldn't say. She allowed herself to be pulled along, his words echoing strangely in her mind. She saw clearly that everything about her marriage was a lie, and that she was alone. As they passed the lady on the cod-liver oil advertisement it seemed to Martha that she too was kibing at her, with her yawnecked smile.

All around Martha there was a jumble of things, posters, pot-holes, pigeons and navvies, and a series of windows, reflecting Charles and Martha walking.

When they turned into Francisco Street, Charles paused before the shop.

– Martha, he said.

Without looking at him Martha could see the lines and hollows of his face.

– I want – I mean, Charles said, you do know that – so far as I have ever loved anyone – I love you.

Martha looked up at the street-lamp nearest the shop. A fine rain was starting, and it fell around the lamp in a spray of light.

– You do know that, Charles said, don't you?

Dreams are our lamps on rainy nights, Martha thought, and she clasped her hands together, rubbing her thumbs into the palms as if polishing them. She could remember, at times, the impression of light streaming upwards from her palms, as though, if she were to clasp her hands round Charles's head she might heal him herself, but she was always afraid. Afraid of what might happen, of what Charles might think.

Charles waited a long moment, then he stepped forward in a bent and shrunken way to unlock the door. Martha saw them both clearly in the dark window, then just herself. It was like looking into the past, or the future. And it came to Martha in that moment that she was free, that she had seen her own life fully, and was free. She stood alone on the pavement and shivered with the sense of freedom.

Then Charles turned to her, and he held out his hand and smiled, and the rare sweetness that was in him sometimes shone through like an angel shining through dark glass.

CHAPTER 15

Louise

I am wide awake and staring in the middle of the night.

Flashing lights, screeching brakes, impact. Then the lurch off the bridge to the river below.

Gradually I return to myself. There is sweat on my upper lip and I'm not breathing properly. I get up and make myself a drink.

The elder taps on the kitchen window as if asking for its flower-heads back. Rain strikes the pane lengthwise. Wind and rain. Just like the night on the bridge.

The new, domestic me has failed to provide cocoa. I make coffee and carry it into the lounge.

There, where I left it, is the album.

Hopeless, I tell myself. Wild-goose chase. Why should I care what happened to her?

Just because it's easier than thinking about what has happened to me.

I get up, go back to the kitchen, move pots.

It's quite spooky, being here alone. If I let myself think about it I could get quite spooked.

Calm down, I tell myself. Go back into the lounge, switch the telly on. Then I curse myself for not having a telly, for not buying more cigarettes, for coming here in the first place.

I miss London. Crazy to leave the city. I'm a city person. I love it for all the reasons my mother hated it, even the dirt. And the vertigo you get when you look up and see one business piled on top of another, the endless pushing, pressing crowds, those discontinuous glimpses of other people's lives.

I let my mother think I was suffering, living there, because it won me a kind of approval. There was nothing my mother approved of more than people making the best of a bad job. When I said I couldn't visit she was sympathetic, if anything. She couldn't imagine anyone wanting to be there, in that noisy, crowded place.

I did visit. Tearing up the motorway after work on a Friday, back down again on Sunday. Not every weekend. When I could.

Sometimes Jamal drove me. All the way there, and back too, when I was weak with grief. And she wouldn't even have him in her room. Even in the extremity of her illness she was quite clear about that. When I first introduced him I could see an endless series of doors swinging shut in her mind. Yet when she died Jamal was there, arranging everything, helping.

When I needed Jamal he was always there. When I didn't he was there too; bursting in on me at work, throwing terrible, jealous scenes. Wanting to examine the whole relationship at three in the morning.

Four years of that was enough. I knew it was over. I invited him round, made sure that this time I stood my ground. He shouted, I cried, the usual.

By the time we wore ourselves out it was three in the morning again. And the one thing I was sure of was that I'd had enough. I was too old for this. I said I would drive him home.

In the car I notice that he is shuddering.

– Jamal, I say. – Come on.

He says nothing. And I don't want to go into it any more. He's a young man, I tell myself. Eight years younger than me. He'll get over it. I fix my poached eyes on the road and keep driving. All the way to the bridge. Which is where he turns to me and says, The end of the road.

– Hm? I say, smiling foolishly, thinking he is maybe giving me directions. When he wrenches the steering-wheel from me I swear I remember a flash of light. Either the Angel of the Lord has descended, or suddenly I know Jamal isn't telling me the way to his house.

I remember struggling in a panic for the wheel. Then a small part of me went cold and still. I let go of the wheel, and, trusting to God and my air-bag, ram my foot down on the accelerator.

Impact.

Then the plunge, which in my mind goes on for ever, every time I close my eyes.

The air-bag does what it's supposed to do, so loudly that I'm left with a hideous pain in both ears. It can't save me from massive bruising, or near drowning, though happily the river is shallow here.

Even so, Jamal is dead and I am not, a point made frequently by the police in their many interrogations. Jamal died from a brain haemorrhage on impact.

– He wrenched the wheel away from me, I tell them.

– He drove the car off the bridge.

I stick to this story despite my strong sense that they can smell the truth on me, or see it like a stain.

Eventually it's over, fingerprints taken, Jamal's unstable past (the harassment of at least one other girlfriend long after she had finished with him) investigated. No charges are made.

I'm free. Free to go home to the silence of my flat, to lie in bed at night and listen to the appalling beating of my heart.

The second night at home Jamal's mother came to the door.

– What did you do to my son, she said.

– I loved him, I said, edging away from her. – He tried to kill me.

I have two memories of what followed.

In the first, while she tells me I'm filth, a filthy whore, using younger men and casting them aside, and that I'm old, too old for these filthy games, I scream at her. – Get out, I say. She doesn't know what she's talking about, she doesn't know what kind of a man he was. And what kind of a mother was she, making her bastard son so twisted?

In the second I say nothing, but put my head in my hands and weep. And eventually we cry in one another's arms, and it is strangely like crying with Jamal.

– My baby, she cries, rocking me, my baby.

When my injuries heal I go back to work. I manage pretty well, very well I think, until one day the boss calls me in, tells me he thinks I could do with some more time off. It's true that I still can't manage to drive, that whenever I stand or even sit still for a moment, I have the sensation of fall. When friends gave a party to celebrate my recovery, I had to edge all the way round the room because I couldn't trust the floor.

Friends soon stopped calling, of course. Even Sally, the woman I could describe as my best friend. Once I saw her, sitting alone in the coffee shop where we usually met. When I joined her, when I sat in front of her, she talked and laughed very rapidly, and I could see fear coming off her like a kind of smoke. It was as if she expected me to fall to the floor any moment and start banging my head, or to cry very loudly, like a child.

Anyway, there were all these unused holidays. And the last of my mother's boxes.

So I returned to Broadstones, though I remembered, many times, saying I would never return. I returned to be the dutiful daughter, doing the last few jobs for my mother. And to lie in bed alone here, once more listening to my heart.

My heart tells me that what I did to Jamal puts me outside the law, outside society. It is something I can never talk about, to anyone.

It tells me this despite the best reasoning of my head, which argues that I was in danger, that I did the best I could. But in the end I cannot know what Jamal intended to do, I can only know my own intentions.

And in that moment I intended to kill him.

Cold on the couch I move stiffly, with a sensation like trying to rouse myself from a heavy dream. It comes to me that I had reached a point with Jamal where I could either open up to him or turn away. And I turned. As I have always done.

My feet are cold. I sit up slowly, hold them in my hands, flex the toes.

I miss him, I think.

I miss him.

My heart and all my body aches. But the way it ended changed everything that ever happened between us.

What do you do when there is nothing in your past you want to remember?

There, on the table where I left it, is the album. Next to the whisky I bought on the way back from Mrs Stowe.

The fall I had saved me, she said.

How foolish to be so shaken by a malicious old woman trying to impress. She probably used the word 'fall' in the biblical sense.

I stare at the album without opening it, think once again about the girl who resembles me. I wonder how she died – bowel cancer, heart failure, brain haemorrhage. Those are just the kinds of death I know.

How much of her death was already in her when the photo was taken?

My feet are numb. I try walking on them experimentally, since there is nothing else to do, backwards and forwards, hugging myself, into the kitchen.

More memories surface as if the movement kindles them, the angle of Jamal's head in the car, the consultant's face when he told me my mother had cancer, Sally's face when I went over to her table, going to the toilet afterwards to smoke and cry.

The thing is, I needn't go back. I could get rid of the flat in London and rent something a third of the price up here.

Then who would I be?

I can hardly feel my feet, and this makes me think suddenly and vividly of Mrs Stowe, and her two dead legs, imagine what it is like to be part corpse. Then it comes to me suddenly, the feeling I have been aware of in odd moments since Jamal died. A kind of impulse in my flesh, in the cells of my flesh, towards dying. Nothing I can talk myself out of, or resist. It is simply there.

It comes to me that part of the feeling I have for my mother, and father, and Jamal, and all the dead people I know, even the girl on the photo, is envy. They've done it now, I have it to do.

It is too hard to live like this.

To distract myself I decide to try just a little of the elderflower wine. I unscrew the top of the bottle with great caution, but the wine doesn't fizz. And it doesn't taste like alcohol to me.

Suddenly I lean over the sink as if I'm going to be sick, gripping the surfaces on either side.

I am Louise Kenworthy, I think, but I can't think my way to the end of the sentence.

The window is like a big black mirror, in which I can only see myself, and the room behind. I stare at myself a moment, then cross the room and turn off the light.

When I return to the window I can see, after a moment, that the darkness is layered, not blank and opaque. All the tortuous, convoluted shapes of foliage are darker than the background darkness. When I look up into the sky it is very deep, like a bowl, but in the garden everything is minute and complicated. I can almost hear the tangling of undergrowth, and all the creeping, gnawing creatures that live in it. I would like to be out there, in the feathery, silvery grass, but I feel too small. Out there creatures I can't name are moving about in their little worlds, one world layered upon another in the teeming, infinite darkness.

CHAPTER 16

My phone is ringing.

Even before I open my eyes I can see orange light through my eyelids. When I prise them apart the sun bores into my eyes. The old tablecloth I have rigged up over the window in order to delay the process of waking up has fallen down.

My phone is still ringing.

It must be morning.

– Did I wake you up? Dan says.

– What time is it?

– Nearly eight.

– Jesus.

– I have to go into work, he says, but listen. I bumped into Frank again the other day. And he said he'd remembered something for you. A newspaper cutting. About Millicent's daughter – Eveline.

– Who?

– Millicent, he says patiently, while my brain clicks gradually into gear. – She had two daughters, Eveline and Laura. And Eveline's still alive.

By now my brain is functioning sufficiently to do sums.

– She can't be, I say.

– The oldest woman in the borough, says Dan, one hundred and three years old. That's what the article's about.

– You're kidding.

– And living in a home not far from here. So if you're interested we could go this afternoon. I have to call in work, but I'll be knocking off at two. OK? There is a buzzing noise down the phone.

– Are you shaving? I say.

– Yep. Got to go. I'll pick you up around three – OK?

I'm left holding the phone.

For some moments I stare at the ceiling, reflecting a little moodily that the only other time my phone rang it was also Dan. In between I have almost forgotten the sound. No one from London has rung. At first I waited for this, restraining myself from making the first call, then gradually I forgot to wait. It is astonishing, I reflect, how quickly it's possible to be erased, from sight and mind.

It was nice of Dan to ring, though, I think. Especially after last time. I thought he'd fallen out with me.

Slowly I assimilate the new information. Millicent's daughter, alive. Mentally I place her in the family tree.

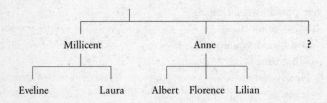

Albert had Thomas, Dan's father, and also Evelyn, I remember, Dan's aunt. I met her once at some family gathering. So the names in our family come and go, come and go. But I still don't know the younger sister's name. And though I have almost persuaded myself that I am no longer interested in the girl in the photograph, that I have been using her as a kind of distraction, still I feel it would be something, after all this time, to know her name.

I move about the house restlessly, picking up clothes and putting them down again.

Eveline must know something about her mother's sister, I think, even if it is only her name.

I pick up more clothes, wondering foolishly what to wear when I visit her.

They all want washing.

In a fit of industry I dump a great pile into the sink and scrub them vigorously with soap.

After all, there may be, I think, pegging out some articles and draping others over the branches of the elder, there may be, now, a moment of truth.

By the time I'm finishing pegging out I can see this is a ridiculous notion. There is no reason at all why Eveline should remember. At her age it would be remarkable if she remembered her own name, let alone her aunt's. I peg out the last shirt, which flaps and billows.

Eveline might have died since the article, I think.

I return to the house, trying to imagine what it must be like to be a hundred and three, to outlive everyone you know, maybe even your own children.

I try, but fail to imagine what this might mean.

As I brew up it occurs to me that Mary didn't follow me into the garden.

She'll be out later, I think.

I'm more settled now that I've done something, composed in mind, sure that this will be yet another blind alley. I rummage in the cupboards for food. Tinned carrots, tinned tomatoes, tinned peas. And garlic from Mary, who always keeps some growing because of her catarrh. I wonder if garam masala has any medicinal use, since what I really fancy is a curry. I allow my mind to dwell lovingly on the food shops in London, the haloumi cheese, the olive pâté, and all the varieties of bread and oil.

The last time I went to the shop down the road there was an old man trying to buy lager. He shook all the time and was 30p short. Tracey and Cath exchanged glances, united for once, stood firm. I had an impulse to give him the money. Not generosity, more like, let everyone die their own way.

This time as I push open the door, Cath is saying, Well, if she wants a row she can come here herself, then she breaks off abruptly and they both glare at me. I don't feel like summoning a smile this time. I walk right past them to the nearest shelf, search unsuccessfully for rice, chilli peppers, cumin. Today the entire shop seems to be stocked with dog food and worming pellets. Cath moves along the shelves after me, conspicuously rearranging what stock there is. Eventually I find baking powder and bleach and drop the money on the desk on the way out.

I can be truculent too.

In fact, as I walk back to the cottage I feel an irritable depression setting in. My thoughts circle like vultures round the memory that kept me awake all night. For the first time I realize how much energy I expend fending them off.

It is no comfort to me that no one knows what I did. The memory I have sits in me like a stone. Ever since that night it has weighted me down. My perceptions since then, the contours of my life, the shape of the time I am walking through, are all pulled by the weight of what I carry inside me, as if drawn along a different axis.

Mary, I think, before I collapse entirely into depression. I could go and talk to Mary.

This is the first time I have knocked on her door, and I feel a prickle of anxiety about it that I tell myself is concern for Mary. I tell myself this and all the black gladioli along her fence shake their heads at me together.

– What is it? Mary says.

Relief. I am relieved to hear the voice of this woman I hardly know.

– Mary, it's Louise, I say. – I didn't see you this morning and I was wondering – I just thought I'd check . . .

– Oh. Come in.

Most of Mary's kitchen is taken up by a table. She sits at the far side of it, managing to look both suspicious and welcoming at once.

– Did you think I were dead? she says.

– Oh, no, I protest, with the emphasis of one determined to say the right thing. – Mind you, I add, in the arch, cajoling tone people customarily use with the elderly, and that irritates me even as I speak, I did think, If Mary's not in her garden, something's not right.

– Sit down, she says.

I sit.

– You don't talk as if you're from round here, she says, as if considering me afresh.

– No, I say, remembering all the painstaking efforts I made to stop talking that way. I look down at my fingers. Mary says nothing.

There is a carnal, fatty smell, which I trace to a pan of brown stuff on the stove, meaty, full of tubes. Looks like lung.

– Bedlam spit, says Mary. – Stay and have some.

– I don't eat meat, I lie.

– Oh. One of them. No wonder you look like a ghost. Have a cup of tea, then. She gets up, putting the kettle on the other burner, extracting a mug and a bowl from the pile of washing-up. I tell her about the shop and we deplore it together, then as she dishes up brown stuff I admire her gladioli, and we discuss winter gardening. Jasmine, viburnum, cyclamen – nothing cheers you up like flowers in winter.

We are talking about winter and all around us the summer is like fire. Yet in my garden the dandelions, thistles and rosebay willowherb are already turning to snowy tufts, the first berries are appearing on the elder, and all of nature is caught up in this intricate orchestration of timings.

– Well, I'm glad to see you're well, I say, sipping the surprisingly good tea Mary has made. – When I didn't see you in the garden I was just a bit worried, that's all.

– I've been in all morning, Mary says, thinking.

– Oh?

– My husband died around this time.

– Oh. I'm sorry.

She tells me a little about her marriage while champing and sucking on the tubular meat so that juices flow down her chin.

– He were a noisy man, she says, of their forty-seven years together, a terrible noisy man.

– In fact, she says, removing a clump of gristle from her teeth, I always seem to lose someone at this time. My mother. The baby.

– The baby?

I only know of one son, improbably called Theodore Butterworth. But Mary nods.

– I had another one after Ted, she says, Frederick.

I try not to smile, but Mary grins through the tubes and gristle.

– Ted and Fred, she says. – It were Cyril's idea.

Then she sighs.

– He were a lovely little lad, she says, not like Ted, always whingeing and mithering on. I'd go into his room wondering why he was so quiet. And do you know what he was doing?

I shake my head.

– Just looking. He used to look at things for hours, waving his little arms and legs about. Leaves through the window, shadows, bits of dust floating around . . . She trails off.

I nod, and an image arises inside me of the room with its wooden cot, the deep mullioned window letting in little light, the stir of tiny hands and feet.

– One day I went in and he were gone, she says. – Nothing prepared me for it, no one could tell me owt. Some memories go but not that one. She sighs heavily and her eyes are moist.

– Even after all this time it'll come on me suddenly and it's like being hit, she says, and this is so close to what I've been thinking that I am wincing inside.

– For months I went around as though there were a hole in my middle where my baby used to be. Then, just this morning, I thought to myself, He had as much life as anyone else.

This is too enigmatic for me. I sip my tea carefully.

– He laughed and cried and suffered things, oh, yes, says Mary, and I don't like to look at the pain in her eyes. – And he did all of that looking. Well. You can't measure life in years, can you? There's no great virtue in living seventy years instead of one. She gets up suddenly and lets her plate and mug clatter into the pot sink.

– He knew what life was, she says, and she looks up from the sink to the window, where scarlet geraniums flatten themselves against the pane like tiny flags.

I feel a pressure in my heart. I want to ask Mary what it's like to have known so many deaths, so that more of the people you have loved are dead than alive. Does one death release another slowly, like releasing balloons into the sky? Does death transform your memory rather than freezing it for ever? Does it make it easier to die?

But Mary is blowing her nose vigorously into the tea-towel, then wiping the gravy from her chin.

– They say your memory goes when you get older, she says. – But it doesn't go. It changes. I can remember all sorts I never could. It changes, that's all. Just like your body changes.

Maybe my memory will change, I think. It is a comforting thought, like a small flame.

– Look at us, Mary says, blowing her nose again, and I manage a pallid smile. – A lovely day like this. And all we can talk about is death.

Ever since I came back to the countryside I've been thinking about death. But where better? I think, remembering the long baying of sheep through the night when the lambs were taken, the bellowing of cows, as if they would turn themselves inside out for their young.

– Have you seen that young man recently? Mary says.

– What young man?

– The one with the car.

I realize she means Dan.

– He phoned me this morning, as a matter of fact. He's calling by this afternoon.

– He's keen, says Mary.

I laugh in denial. And realize simultaneously that it's true.

– I can tell, Mary says.

I don't ask her how she can tell, when her acquaintance with our relationship must be limited to what she can see from her window. I stop laughing, regard her gravely.

– If that's true, Mary, I say, maybe I should warn him off now.

– Get on with you.

I'm serious.

– We could all say that, Mary says, beginning to dry the pots with the same towel she has blown her nose on. For a moment I feel an almost unbearable compulsion to tell her everything, to lay my head on her elderly breast and indulge in the comfort of confession.

– I killed a man once, I could say.

Instead I tell her where we are planning to go and why. It occurs to me that I should have done this weeks ago, that if anyone could remember the labyrinthine relationships of the locality it would be Mary. But she shakes her head. She has seen the newspaper article, she says, but she didn't recognize the name.

– Not from round here, she says.

Which is interesting in itself.

As I leave Mary presses fennel and nutmeg on me. I take them back, add them to the tinned ingredients, make a soup.

Then, even though I'm not interested in Dan, and have just laughed at Mary's claim, I wash and change into the smartest clothes I have here, apply makeup. It's good of him to take me, I tell myself, after the near falling-out we had last time. Carefully I extract the photograph from the album, and wait for him to arrive.

CHAPTER 17

We drive to the home in almost total silence. It is as if what Mary said has paralysed the muscles of my throat. Dan makes a few comments, then stares straight ahead, and when I think he won't notice, I manage a quick sideways glance, taking in the sagging jawline, the uneven, greying bristliness of his skin, the broken veins, the puffiness around the eyes.

Even so he is not unattractive, though I am not attracted to him. He isn't Paul, of course. Or Jamal. Yet I'm reduced to this foolish silence, like a girl. Fortunately the drive isn't a long one.

The Autumn Prospect Retirement Home is a low modern building, well-kept lawns dotted with benches. Inside, the walls are a uniform pale green and none of the doors shut.

– So they can't lock themselves in, the nurse explains.

As she takes us towards Eveline's room we see another nurse leading an old man by the hand. He is bent nearly double, his lower lip hanging.

– Whatever shall I do, he groans, whatever shall I do?

– This is Mrs Crowther's room, our nurse says.

And the door opens.

There is a bed with a crucifix above it, and a pale green leather chair with wooden armrests.

And in the chair there is Eveline.

At first sight she reminds me of one of the begonias in my London flat, the mottled, crinkled texture of her skin, the dilapidated air. Her limbs are disposed rather awkwardly around the chair, as if parts of her might wither and fall, very gently and gracefully, to the floor.

Only her hands, immense and meaty, contradict this overall impression of great fragility.

Her expression doesn't change as we approach. She has a long, mournful nose and greyish, scrappy hair. Her eyes are camouflaged against the spotted flesh of her face. They are filmy, like the eyes of a newborn child.

– Visitors for you, says the nurse quite loudly, rearranging the cushions of Eveline's chair.

– Can she hear? I say.

Oh, yes. She's a bit forgetful, but she's sharp enough, aren't you, Evie? she says loudly to Eveline, who ignores her. – You'll have to explain who you are, she says to us.

The nurse departs. I sit on the edge of the bed, facing Eveline, who blinks very slowly. We explain several times who we are and I show her the photograph.

– Martha, she says at once, in a voice like the rustling of crispy leaves.

Somewhere deep inside me a bell chimes.

– Did you know her?

– It was a long time ago . . .

She hesitates, we wait.

– I'd like to know about her, I say, though my heart is tightening and I'm less and less sure that I do want to know.

– Did she die young? I say, in spite of myself. – Did she marry?

– We've got a photo of Albert's wedding, you see, says Dan. And your mother's in it but not Martha.

– Yes, says Eveline, looking from one to the other of us with those vague, primordial eyes.

– Perhaps they had a fall-out, I say helpfully.

There is a high, keening noise from one of the other inmates, distracting Eveline.

– I went to see her once, she says, after a moment, when I was quite a little girl. With my mother and my sister Laura. No, not

Laura, she says, scrumpling the material of her skirt, Not Laura, Robert – but Robert wasn't born then – and then he died . . . She looks at us helplessly.

– It's all right, says Dan, in a soothing way. – Take your time.

– She lived above a bookshop, she says, and immediately I can see it in my mind. When I was a little girl I used to want to run a bookshop.

– A dreadful, dark, dingy place, Eveline is saying, and I adjust the image. – With tiny rooms that smelt of damp and cabbages. Auntie Anne was there – your grandmother.

– Great-grandmother, Dan says, making her pause. I glare at him.

– Albert and Jean were my grandparents, he says, oblivious. – Anne and Edward were Albert's parents.

– She was nice to me, Eveline says, smiling at me. – I spilled my drink all down my dress and she said – she said never mind.

She smiles again, very sweetly, and I smile back encouragingly.

– I remember Auntie Anne saying how small it was for the two of them, you know. She was always very outspoken, Auntie Anne.

She smiles again, sadly.

– Martha was married, then? I prompt.

– Oh, yes – yes – I believe so. But it was all so long ago.

Her eyes have a vacant, but troubled look. I feel sorry for her, but Dan is persistent.

– When did she die? he says, and Eveline flinches away.

– Where's my magazine? she mumbles, and her large hands fidget. – They're supposed to bring it every day.

– Nurse! she cries suddenly, startling us. – Has – my – magazine – come – yet?

A young, pretty woman hurries in.

– Now, Mrs Crowther, don't upset yourself. She plumps up the cushions and tries to settle Eveline back into her chair, but Eveline resists with a flapping motion of her great hands. She's larger than the nurse, who settles her with some difficulty.

– Maybe you'd better go now, she says over Eveline's shoulder, but suddenly all the fight goes out of Eveline. She is limp, exhausted.

– No, she says, and it is barely an expulsion of air, no, I'm well. I will be well again, won't I? she says, looking up at the nurse, who tells her that of course she will be, right as rain.

We get up to go. Then Eveline looks directly at me.

– It's not a nice story, she says, and again I feel that peculiar tightening around the heart.

– I don't remember things very well any more, she is saying, but there are letters.

I step forward and the nurse frowns.

– Letters?

– My granddaughter has them. I don't think – she wouldn't mind –

– Where does she live? Dan says.

Eveline looks helplessly up at the nurse.

– She usually comes here on a Sunday, the younger woman says, without looking at us. – Now, Mrs Crowther, I'm going to go and get your medication.

She turns towards us.

– Perhaps you shouldn't stay too long, she says, she's getting tired.

– Of course, we say, but Eveline is fiddling with her purse.

– Here, here you are, she is saying, and a number of papers fall out.

– She wrote it down for me, she says. – In case I ever needed to – you know.

I take the scrap from her, not liking to look at the expression in her eyes. Then stare blankly at it.

Well, why not? I think. Round here everyone seems to be related to everyone else.

Mrs Mary Brennan, it says. 202 Lambs Hill Road, Greenbridge.

Since I already have the address, I put the paper back in her purse and close it for her, make myself look into her eyes and smile. Unexpectedly she puts her hand on mine.

– Don't let her go, she says, but I have the oddest feeling that she's not talking to me at all. I smile and pat her hand, and we leave.

On the way out we pass another nurse leading an old woman to the toilet. As we pass the old lady breaks free and runs towards us.

– My face, she cries, in the greatest excitement, clutching at the loose skin of her cheeks. – What's happened to my face?

– Agnes, Agnes, the nurse says, leading her away. – Sorry about that, she says to us.

I walk a little ahead of Dan and once more have nothing to say. Some bird seems to have its talons round my skull. I'm sorry I ever started this; sorry that I've stirred up Eveline's memories and left her to the mercy of them, because memories have no mercy.

Would I have put my mother in a place like this?

Probably.

And where will I be, in my old age? Already my mind is as full of holes as a cheese, and the unremembered bits of my life have fallen through. And even the bits I can remember slip in and out of the holes, appearing and disappearing, changing all the time. Maybe the holes will get bigger and swallow everything else up.

Here I am, Louise Kenworthy, taking the huge step from being haunted by my past to being haunted by my future.

As Dan opens the car door for me, he says, Do you think you'll phone Eveline's granddaughter?

– No, I say.

CHAPTER 18

– Hello, is that Mrs Mary Brennan?

Funny thing curiosity, gets to be a power on its own.

– Yes?

– My name's Louise Kenworthy. We met recently – at a meeting in your house.

Silence.

– The workhouse, I prompt.

– Oh, yes – yes. Did you get the newsletter?

– No –

– I'm sure I sent you one – I did give you some petition forms, didn't I?

– Yes –

– Only there's an emergency meeting on Thursday night at the council offices. They're up to their usual tricks, she says, holding meetings at little or no notice when they think no one'll get there. Petra's hoping we'll all get there, with all the petitions. She thinks they might take a decision about the workhouse there and then –

– This isn't about the workhouse, I say gently. I take a deep breath. – I've just discovered that we may be related.

Mary is silenced by this.

– I visited your grandmother the other day, I begin.

– She's all right, isn't she? I've been meaning to get there –

– She's fine. I was talking to her about the family tree . . . I explain the connection. Again. Mary Brennan keeps saying, Oh, yes – yes, as if she doesn't understand at all. I feel more than a little foolish.

– She said you have some letters, I conclude weakly. – I mean – I don't want to put you to any trouble –

– Oh, yes – I do have them somewhere.

– Well, if it's any trouble, I repeat, hedging.

– Oh, no – I think I know where they are – that's if – we did out the loft recently – I'll just go and check.

She plods off.

Stupid, I tell myself. Stupid, stupid. Can't leave well alone.

She is gone for some time and I lean against the wall, telling myself to hang up.

– Yes, they're all here, she says, and my stomach twists. – At least – there aren't that many of them – but I think they're all here.

– Can I see them? I say, and my voice is a whisper.

– Of course. You can borrow them if you like – I've never really known what to do with them. But I can't bring myself to throw them out. Shall I send them to you?

I clear my throat.

– I'll call round, I say.

As I wait for Mary to answer the door I reflect on the merry-go-round of social fortunes that the children of Anne and Edward seem to have ridden: down with Albert, up again with Tom and Dan, down with Susan Millicent, up again some of the way with me. But for Millicent's line it looks like a steady slide down, through Eveline to Mary.

Not all the way, of course – this isn't poverty, just respectability on the edge.

Well, who'd've thought it? says Mary, opening the door. – Come in, come in. Her physical appearance has more impact on me this time. I catch myself searching unsuccessfully for traces of family likeness in the plump build and greying-brown hair, the nervous eyes behind their horn rims. She talks all the time, about having done some research into the family tree herself, but that she's hardly an expert, about the family having moved from Harrogate to

Barnsley when she was quite young, then her husband got a job as foreman at the factory in Greenbridge before it closed. Then she talks about the circumstances that led to her grandmother going into the home. Apparently Eveline had stayed with them a while in the downstairs room when they first moved here. Mary was the only relative left but she had three sons, only three bedrooms, not even that, two and a box, and her husband's back's bad.

Obviously in her eyes I'm a judge.

I tell her about my mother's illness, and how hard I found it; she scarcely nods. Then I tell her about the album, and the gaps in it, and that my mother's name was Susan Millicent, and she brightens a little. Her own mother was called Joy, she tells me, Joy Anne, and she died quite young, in her fifties. Eveline had her and a son called Robert Arnold, who died three or four years ago, aged seventy-six. He was called Robert Arnold after Eveline's brother, who died just before he was born. Arnold was a family name as well; Millicent's husband had been called Arnold.

– And Laura? I ask. Eveline's sister?

She died twenty years ago in New Zealand, where the family had emigrated.

Poor Eveline, I think.

Mary knows little about Eveline's parents. As far as she can tell from family photos, Arnold died in middle age, Millicent later on, in her seventies. No one knows where Eveline gets her unreasonable longevity from.

She veers into a tirade against the neighbours, bang bang bang and they knew Eveline wasn't well, so much for the laws about noise, you complain and what do they do about it? Nothing. They were out there now, her neighbours, planting conifers to take up all her light and drain her soil.

– That's why I got involved in the Residents' Association, Mary says.

We are sitting in Mary's kitchen. Sunlight flits across blotchy linoleum, and the sand-coloured panels of her kitchen units. Through the open door I can see the pink pot cats and chintz of her living room. There are more pot cats than I realized the night of the meeting, and Mary hasn't stopped talking yet, she has scarcely drawn breath, and I can see why Eveline might have wanted to go into that home.

Finally, though there is barely a pause, I say weakly, The letters?

– Oh, yes, she says, and disappears.

I stay where I am, meeting the gaze of the nearest pot cat. Then I take a few notes, the names of Eveline's children, of Millicent's husband, and Mary's sons.

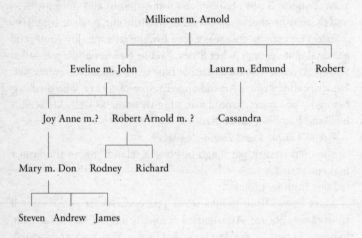

It's still unfinished, of course, perhaps it will always be unfinished. I fill in what I can, and as I write I have the impression that this moment, with its dappled surfaces, sunlight and linoleum and cats, will always exist. I look round again and realize that, pot cats and chintz apart, the house is exactly like my mother's – a large front room and a small kitchen, where I sat on the doorstep always in a square of light. And the sky was always blue. Why is that?

Mary reappears, so entirely out of breath that I have to help her to her stool. She waves a medium-sized brown envelope at me.

– Here they are, she says, and despite my best efforts, my heart lurches again.

– You know that was a terrible business, Mary says eventually. – That poor girl.

This would be the time. I could ask Mary to tell me everything, prepare me. I could hear the worst over a cup of coffee and it might not look so bad. This would be the moment to open my mouth and ask, and I am going to do it, when there is a sudden, horrible banging on the wall.

Mary gasps.

– They're at it again, she says, right after I've asked them, and she flies up the stairs in apparent defiance of gravity. The next minute she's hammering on the wall with the handle of a brush and it seems like a good time to leave.

– I'll see myself out, I say, but she doesn't hear.

Out of the front door again, along the path to the gate. As I close the gate behind me Mary suddenly appears in the doorway. She is mouthing and gesturing. Her face looks ridiculous, like a fish.

– Don't forget about the meeting, she seems to be saying. You'll see why – and she points at the package under my arm, then, as if she has said too much, shuts up her mouth like a trap and disappears.

I walk past the roadworks, up the hill towards the stop where Nigel Scowcroft assailed me that night, where I first felt the presence of my mother. As I walk now I can hear her hectoring voice.

You should never have left Martin.

Why get married when you don't want children?

I want her back, I realize. I want to be taking this envelope back to her. We could read the letters together and it would be all right. Instead of which I'm going back to an empty house that isn't mine, carrying a brown envelope in my hand like a ticking bomb.

CHAPTER 19

There used to be this advert on telly when I was a little girl. It mapped out the course of a headache, from the nape of the neck over the skull. I massage my neck and shoulders but can't get rid of this one. I wonder if it's worthwhile going to the shop, just to find out they don't sell painkillers.

Tension. There's a lot of tension in my face. That was where the white lines on the advert ended.

Funny how memories surface. I couldn't have dredged that one up voluntarily. It floated upwards of its own accord, from the murky pond of my past. How many more of them do I have? All the days I've woken up, happy, miserable, tense, got dressed, cleaned my teeth, walked or driven to my unremarkable destination, where are all those moments now?

Yet some of them float on the surface, like broken bottles. Ever since Mary gave me the envelope I can see in my mind's eye, for no reason at all that I can think of, the back of the consultant's neck as I follow him to the room where he will tell me, finally, about my mother. Reddish folds and ridges overhang his collar, and as I follow them past an interminable series of doors, trolleys and notices and ward windows bob up and down in my peripheral vision, unsteady in the quivering light. By the time we get to the Special Room, the one painted in peach and aqua as though done over by one of those television teams, prints of Monet on the walls, the folds and ridges of his neck have told me everything I need to know.

I could go home now. Back to London, and leave the letters here without ever opening them. I could turn this moment round now, and change the moment I'm in for ever, by going home.

I could open the elderflower wine, or walk to the shop for cigarettes.

It's getting dark.

I make a coffee and sit down with the envelope. I don't want it to be dark when I read the letters.

CHAPTER 20

There are six letters. The first, dated 4 April 1904, is from Millicent to Anne, in the same spidery script I have found on the back of photographs. The details are practical, the tone one of uncomprehending pain. *They are saying*, she writes, *that the attic door was locked from the <u>outside</u>. They are implying cruel and outrageous things . . .*

I read this letter twice before the significance of it sinks in. There was a fire. It started in the attic. The remains of Martha's husband were found in the attic. Martha's husband was called Charles. No trace of Martha was found.

When I have finished reading it twice I stare blankly at the wall.

Oh, my God, I think. She killed him.

This is it, I think. This is what I have been waiting to hear.

It is some time before I pick up the second letter, dated 6 June 1904. It is from the insurance firm, briefly and formally regretting that in cases of arson no remittance is possible.

The third, dated 13 June 1904, is another letter from Millicent to Anne. She encloses two letters, she writes, one from the insurance firm and one from the mortgage company, which is one that no one has ever heard of. Arnold cannot find them in any directory, his associates know nothing about them. But they are claiming the rights to what remains of the property and stock.

I look in vain for this letter; it is not in the envelope.

. . . There seems to be no will [she writes]. *In any case, surely*

Martha would be the beneficiary. And there is still no word of Martha. The police continue their enquiries, Arnold has been tireless in his. I have tried to trace Charles' family, but there are no records of a Charles Wrigley, or an Enoch Wrigley. Why would there be no records?

It is almost as if the relationship was a false one, but there is nothing else to tell us where Charles did come from . . .

Next there is a brief letter from Anne, dated 2 August 1904.

I share your grief about our sister. And certainly if she were to appear now I should have something to say to her. But I must beg you not to keep writing in this way. Since Father has lived with us he has not been well and grows increasingly confused. I conceal from him what I can, and only hope that you will not write to him directly. It seems to me now that wherever Martha is, she has taken certain things upon herself and cannot be helped. It seems to me that the best we can do is to put this calamity behind us . . .

There is a short reply to this from Millicent, dated 16 August 1904.

Naturally I will respect your wishes [she writes]. *Certainly I would do nothing to increase our father's distress. But as for forgetting our sister, that I cannot do. I cannot stop thinking about her. When I go to sleep at night, when I wake in the morning, she is there in my mind. I cannot stop imagining the worst. It seems to me* [she concludes] *that it would almost be better to know that she was dead than this . . .*

I hold these two letters in my hands, looking at the contrast between Millicent's spidery handwriting and Anne's bold copperplate. It seems plain to me that Millicent has the kind of mind that cannot let a thing go until she has understood it thoroughly. Not unlike my mother, I think.

That ends the correspondence between Millicent and Anne. The last letter, dated 19 February 1938, is from Millicent to Eveline. *I still think about her every day,* she writes. *I have never given up hope.*

And then she mentions the prisons and asylums she has visited, the corpses she has viewed. *It was not a pleasant task,* she writes, *but I believed that it had to be done. Mainly I hoped that some workhouse might have taken her in . . .*

She travelled from one workhouse to another, from Broadstones to Rochdale and Wakefield, from Bolton to Preston, in the hope of finding Martha.

> *There was no great cruelty* [she writes]. *Only that the little ones were not allowed to play. Twice a day they were lined up in the yard for air, but had to stay in line and not move about. And when I asked the Matron she said it was so their costume should not be spoiled.*
>
> *Can it not be washed? I said. And mended? And she gave me a sour look, but I wrote to the Board . . .*

And so years of campaigning began. She campaigned for the children to be taught at the nearest school, where they could play with other children, and raised funds for them to have ordinary clothes to wear so that they should not stand out in 'workhouse blue'. She campaigned for better inspection of the workhouses themselves. She wrote to newspapers, harassed MPs.

Her next words make me sit very still, staring at the page.

> *It finally came to me that if there were no records of Charles' birth, and no relatives, that he might have been born in one of these places, and I retraced my steps, but with no result. Either records had been lost or stolen or hidden away, but I never saw them . . .*

I am thinking about Charles, and Emma Whately. I think for so long that the coffee I have made for myself goes cold. I could check this, I think. I could go to the library and check. And this one small detail would make a world of stories fall into place. I stare at the cooker, as if it will tell me a secret, then eventually I read on.

And now it's over [she writes], *and the last workhouse closed, ending a dark chapter in our history, though an even darker one seems to be beginning. And still no news of Martha. She would be fifty-one years old this coming month.*

I cannot any longer suppose her alive. It is one of the three great sorrows of my life. Along with the deaths of Robert, and your father. But if I had to choose which was the sharper pain I would still say that not to know is hardest . . .

I sit for some time thinking about this woman, Millicent, for whom death, Charles's death and the loss of her sister, became a journey; who turned into one of those many unknown women who worked for something, and made a difference. And I think of Martha disappearing, erased from the family tree, no one named after her. Maybe she married again and had children, maybe she died. I think of her becoming a powerful absence.

And I think about death being at the centre, and the journeys people take radiating out from it, the mysterious trajectories of people's lives.

Death at the heart of everything, fuelling all the stories of the world.

And I think about my own story, which is both a continuation of Martha's and a departure from it, and how all the time I seem to have been journeying backwards: back to my mother and the family line.

CHAPTER 21

I find what I am looking for right away. There, in the entries for 1871: Emma Whately, pauper, (d.), Charles her son.

Charles her son.

It means nothing, necessarily.

It means everything.

It means I have a story to tell.

I flick back and forwards through the records. It's easy when you know what you're looking for. An Emma Whately is registered in 1870, but not before. In 1882 Charles was apprenticed to one Enoch Wrigley, bookseller. He seems to have taken on Enoch Wrigley's name.

All the time I'm checking the records I'm also aware of the front desk, waiting for Paul to come in. It would be nice to share this with him, apart from anything. It might certainly be a story he could use. I stay in the reference room quite a while, sketching it out, fitting Mrs Stowe's story together with Millicent's. It seems to me that they make a kind of circle, beginning and ending with the workhouse, taking in Martha along the way. I imagine that Martha may have ended up in the workhouse, but that's just imagination, filling in the gaps.

Then there's Henry Hawkyard's story.

I realize that I want the stories to fit together very much. But why? For Paul?

Each way I sketch the story out I'm dissatisfied. I can't find the right language to tell it in, given that my language is so different from Martha's, or Emma's, or Alice's. And there are still too many gaps. I'm not sure where to look next, or if looking further would be useful. I could go to the County Records Office in Manchester and try to find out more about the bookshop – but would that help? Around all research you have to draw a line. I have to draw my own line, for myself.

I leave my notes unfinished and turn to my family tree. More gaps. Martha, of course, but also Maybelline's children, Cora and Victor, Eveline's sister, Laura, her brother Robert, Albert's sister, Florence, Tom's sister, Evelyn. It's like looking at a map of the dark side of the moon, or maps that early explorers used, when they had to fill in the details as they went.

I get tired of looking at loose ends, tired of looking up every time someone opens the door. I yawn and stretch and pack my bag.

After this inconclusive beginning I have an inconclusive day. I wander round the shops looking for a present for Mary. Because I think now that I'm ready to leave. Or, at least, that there isn't much more for me to do here, that back in London I will come to a decision about my job and my flat.

But what should I get for Mary? I consider dried flowers, then a battered radio. But she already has a radio, large, unwieldy and sizzling though it is. She says it was her mother's.

I go from one shop to another, looking at brass ornaments and mangles. People nod at me here and there, I spend time talking in shops. Martha became a stranger, I think, I have stopped being one.

Eventually, failing to take a decision about Mary's present, I buy a bottle of wine for myself and return to the cottage.

A flyer has been pushed through my door.

URGENT, it says at the top in red, then

ACTION in blue, and

DON'T LET THEM GET AWAY WITH IT in lime green. Beneath are the details of the council meeting Mary Brennan told me about.

MAKE YOUR VOICE HEARD, it says in orange.

Ordinarily I would crumple it up and throw it at the bin. Instead I stand behind my front door, reading the small print. Attend Thursday, 6 p.m., it says.

All right, I think. Yes.

Today is Thursday. I'm tired, but in the light of everything I've found out, I can't just ignore the fate of the workhouse. I consider taking the letters back to Mary at the meeting, then I decide to ask if I can keep them a while longer, take copies, maybe show them to Paul.

Paul will be impressed, I think.

Most of all, as the afternoon ticks on, I consider Martha. Where on earth did she get to? I wonder. How on earth did she survive? I have images of her begging, turning to prostitution. I have images of her moving to a different town, changing her name, getting married again, raising half a dozen kids. Probably just down the road from here, I think. Nothing would surprise me now. I could be related to Tracey, or Cath, Mary next door, Nigel Scowcroft, even Paul. Then I imagine a meeting finally between Martha and Millicent, when they were very old.

Millicent: Is that you, Martha?

Martha: Mill?

I sweep the floor and wipe down surfaces in the kitchen.

Trying to find out everything is like trying to build a house without spaces for the rooms, or windows, I think, and Martha is there, suddenly, at one window then another. She is waving to me from the spaces.

I clear leaves from the grid outside and pour bleach down it. Then for the first time since coming here I use my mobile. I phone Mary Brennan, to say that I will definitely come to the meeting and to ask her if she wants the letters back right away. When I tell her that Paul might be able to use them she says I am welcome, and not to bother. It is as though a burden has fallen from her. Then I phone the library and leave a message for Paul, to say that I will be calling by in the next day or so with the results of my research. I leave my phone number in case he needs to tell me he won't be in. Still feeling bold, I phone Dan, but he's out. Then I slip on a jacket, apply lipstick, set off towards the bus stop.

It has moved again, a black bin bag tied carefully around the top of the old one (who does that?). It has been a long time since I walked towards the town centre. The roadworks have gone forth and multiplied if anything, no sign of the work being finished. I follow the line of them along Whittaker Street and up Kicker Brew, and eventually find a group of people standing unhopefully around a pole.

– Is this the bus stop? I ask.

They don't know.

I wait with them. There is a young man who paces backwards and forwards, then hops from one foot to the other; an older woman who sways as though rocking a child to sleep. I jiggle and tap my foot nervously. Only the old man stands like a statue, eyes fixed unswervingly on the distance.

I could call a taxi, I think. Or even walk. Yet I hover, feeling a kind of group pressure and expectancy, the primitive power of old gathering places. If enough people gather round a pole, it seems to suggest, they might *make* a bus appear.

Then astonishingly one does, weaving a slow course through the orange ribbons and cones decorating the road. Tension sags out of our waiting group, though as we gather round to board the old man goes so far as to say that in his day buses ran to time.

The driver's bloodshot eyes ignite.

– And when were that, eh? he shouts. – When they had horse-drawn trams?

– *Eh!* says the old man, but the driver wants to know if we'd like his job, because if we would we're welcome. We can try crawling from one set of traffic lights to another all day, then getting flak for being late. Do we know how much he's paid?

– I'm just saying – begins the old man.

– WELL, DON'T, GRANDAD, bellows the driver, and the old man bridles like a badger, but the swaying woman says, Can't we just get *on*? And we all make our way to a seat, the old man asking us all the way if we've heard what the driver said.

– *Bastard*, says the driver as someone slips round him.

– Did you hear that? the old man demands.

Then the driver has to turn into a street, but no one will let him in.

– Jesus, Jesus, Jesus, he says, and for a moment I think I see him bang his head on the steering-wheel.

– He's dangerous, the old man says to me.

We lurch round a hair-pin bend and I clutch the seat in front.

– Shouldn't be allowed to drive, the old man says, a little too loudly, and I hold my breath. The driver wrenches his brakes on and everyone plunges forward. There is muttering and unrest along the bus. We turn into the main road, crawling now, roadworks on both sides.

Croping, my mother's voice says. Croping and crappling. Do better walking. And, in fact, pedestrians are overtaking us. So at the next stop, where a number of people get off, I get off too, though it is two stops early. Behind me the old man ostentatiously notes down the driver's number.

– Here, take it, the driver says. – You can have the badge too. And the hat.

The evening is noticeably cool. Late now, I hurry past the giant earthworm of traffic inching its way towards the town centre, the women with clipboards trying to get me to fill in a form. Someone hands me a leaflet on hairdressing, pigeons rise, flapping in front of me, and I reach the side door of the town hall.

Someone is already speaking by the time I find the room.

– And the way I see it, he is saying, it seems only common sense to make use of the resources already available.

I slip into a row of chairs, removing my jacket as unobtrusively as possible.

The room is a beige oblong. It contains posters for the CPSA and UNISON, four rows of plastic chairs and a table long enough to seat twenty people, though in fact only five sit round it. Councillor

Norris and Irene Travis are at one end, facing a man and a woman I don't know, and the man who is speaking sits part-way along.

When he finishes, the woman, a lock of fairish hair bobbing in front of her, says, You're *not* referring to those *monstrous* effigies of Native Americans that have suddenly sprouted all over the borough? And a ripple of laughter runs around the room.

I check the audience, which seems to consist almost entirely of members of the Blackshaw and Harrop Residents' Association, though only a few members have made it. Petra Willis and Mary Brennan sit together on the front row, very erect in identical hats, and Les is at the back. He flexes his long fingers at me momentarily in greeting. George is on the row in front of me, and on the same row, further along, there is an elderly couple I haven't seen before.

Then I notice Nigel Scowcroft, on the same row as me, winking and nodding as if we are old friends. I acknowledge him briefly and to my alarm he makes a sudden sideways movement with the speed of a gecko, darting along the row towards me.

– That's Shirley Shaw, he whispers loudly, nodding towards the woman who has just spoken. I glare at him.

– Gerald Armitage, he adds, indicating the man who was speaking as I came in.

Gerald Armitage has a large red face and a smile as wide as a frog's. Momentarily thwarted, he spreads his enormous hands and raises his shoulders and eyebrows simultaneously, until he looks like a picture of Humpty Dumpty I used to have in a book when I was very small.

– Well, I don't see – he begins.

– I'm afraid my residents feel that we have enough renditions of Native Americans in the borough already, for no good reason that anyone can think of.

There is a faint hear-hear from the elderly couple, and Nigel Scowcroft leans towards me again.

– *Councillor* Shirley Shaw, he mouths. I turn my face away.

Gerald Armitage's face darkens.

– I was just making the point – he begins, but again Shirley Shaw cuts in.

– I'm afraid my residents don't see the point, she says. – One statue in Hoarstone Park, one in the playing fields, one in Knoll Green, and now one in the market square, of all places. Whoever took them *in*, she says, looking meaningfully at Gerald, obviously bought a job lot *cheap* for some *inexplicable* reason, and has now set about foisting them on innocent residents. Who I may say, she continues loudly, as he tries to interrupt, are of the opinion that he should put them all in his own back garden and play with them himself.

Scattered clapping from the Residents' Association, and my peripheral vision tells me that Nigel Scowcroft is nodding, beaming and winking at me again.

Gerald Armitage begins to bluster, but then the other man interrupts him. Without moving his long head from his long hands, or opening his eyes, which seem permanently closed, he speaks in a drawn-out voice.

– I think we should keep to the matter in hand. Which is, of course, related to the tourist industry, and the proposed development of traditional sites. Including the building once known as the District Workhouse.

He presses his long fingers together and waits.

– Barry Siddall, whispers Nigel hoarsely, and he starts to tell me something else, but Barry Siddall says, Perhaps Councillor Norris would read the proposals.

Up jumps Councillor Norris, whisking out papers and passing round copies for other members of the council to see. I notice again what a dapper little man he is, with his thick, immaculate hair and small hands. He looks round with an air of discretion.

– Firstly, he says, the move to turn it into warden accommodation has unfortunately had to be rejected on grounds of access. And the idea of turning it into several small business units has come to nothing for the same reason, and because, sad to say, small business units haven't exactly been thriving in Broadstones lately.

And he looks very regretful indeed.

– The move to turn it into a conference centre has been withdrawn. Most people seem to feel that the Blackshaw Hotel is a better venue – except, of course, for those people who have used it before . . . He pauses for laughter, but Councillor Shaw and Gerald Armitage are muttering at one another and swapping papers around, and Irene Travis, deprived of cigarettes, flicks her pen instead with a movement like flicking ash.

– Just my little joke, he goes on. – There was, briefly, the idea of a theme park, which might have been the ideal opportunity to use up Gerald's statues – a collective groan goes up from the members of the Residents' Association, and Councillor Norris has to raise his voice.

– but again there are problems, with both access and drainage. He pauses.

Barry Siddall raises his eyebrows without opening his eyes.

– Well, that leaves us with your suggestion, Larry, he says to Councillor Norris, and there is an almost palpable sense of expectation amongst the Residents' Association, and Petra and Mary lean forward.

– of handing it over to Boyd.

There is a gasp from Petra, and Councillor Norris shuffles papers very rapidly.

– I wouldn't say it was *my* suggestion, he says, and Petra breaks in, What about the museum? That's the proposal you *said* you were going to support.

Barry Siddall opens his eyes for the first time.

– There never was a proposal to turn it into a museum, he says. – We can't get the funding to run the small museum we've got.

Petra seems to stagger, in a sitting position, and I feel a thrill of shock myself.

– But you *said*, she begins, and Barry Siddall says, I have to remind you that members of the public are allowed only to spectate, not participate.

About forty different expressions charge like horses across Petra's face, but Barry Siddall continues looking at her mildly and she doesn't speak.

– Thank you, Barry, says Councillor Norris. – As I was saying, these aren't really my plans at all. I merely promised to represent them at the meeting, and he takes out his glasses.

– What about what you promised us? says George, and Irene Travis speaks up for the first time.

– I think we've had enough interruptions, she says, looking at Barry Siddall, who says that if there are any more the offending persons will be shown from the room. Nigel Scowcroft tries to catch my eye, but I stare perseveringly at the front.

– The proposal is as follows, says Councillor Norris. Colin Boyd has said that he is willing to invest a considerable sum on the tasteful, and I do mean *tasteful*, conversion of the original building into luxury homes, taking into account the provision of adequate access, drainage, parking facilities, etc. And I must say, he adds, taking off his glasses and looking at Barry Siddall, that some of his ideas are quite ingenious – I've seen most of the plans –

– But it's a *listed building*, Petra says, and Barry Siddall sits forward in his chair.

– I must ask you to conform to the rules of the meeting, he says.

– As I was saying, Councillor Norris goes on, the plans for conversion are both tasteful and ingenious, causing the minimum disruption to the original structure. Mr Boyd has gone to considerable trouble to explain the finer details to Mrs Travis here and myself –

– I'll bet he has, says Petra, and George says, How much did he slip you? and all the councillors look very shocked.

– Do we have to listen to this? says Irene Travis, and Councillor Norris looks at Petra for the first time and says, You're not letting me say anything – how can I explain if you won't let me say anything?

– You've said more than enough, says Petra. She stands and Mary stands with her.

– You're a pack of charlatans, she says.

Then Irene Travis is on her feet, saying that this is a disgrace, and Gerald Armitage says that this isn't getting us anywhere, and Shirley Shaw says that perhaps the meeting should be closed if people can't behave themselves, so that finally Barry Siddall becomes quite animated, and bangs on the table.

– That's enough, he says, all of you.

But Petra raises her stick and jabs it towards Councillor Norris.

– You are *on record*, she says, as saying, at Mrs Brennan's house, that you would give *no support* to private applications of this nature.

– That was before I saw the *plans*, Councillor Norris begins, and Barry Siddall says, That's it now, things have gone far enough.

– You said you'd do everything in your power, *everything* – you're all witnesses, she says, rounding on us and waving her stick.

We nod, looking scared.

– I've had enough of this, says Irene Travis, and Barry Siddall says he's going to call security.

– Don't you worry, Petra says, wheeling round, we're going.

And she directs a final glare at Councillor Norris, who pipes, You're out of order, you know, you really are.

Petra stops in her tracks and seems to swell to almost twice her actual size.

– And you, sir, she says, are a snake in the grass. And with that she turns and leaves, rather magnificently, I think, with Mary Brennan scampering behind.

Once they've gone the tension in the room relaxes suddenly, like the releasing of an elastic band. We stare after her uncertainly, then Barry Siddall says, Shall we continue? And Irene Travis sits down again, and George sinks back in his chair shaking his head.

– *Audire discere*, mutters Nigel Scowcroft at me, but I ignore him.

Councillor Norris replaces his spectacles and finishes going through the plans. Three four-bedroomed houses, six three-bedroomed houses and four bungalows – all with gardens, of course.

That might mean clearing more of the land than the original site, as there would certainly be drainage problems.

The trees, I think, and from nowhere Frank's voice sounds in my mind.

> When wur theau born owd rugged oak
> How many year hast seen?

There is a brief discussion of drainage, and Shirley Shaw wants to know when the plans will be available for public inspection, so that people can object, if they want to, through the proper channels. Then Gerald Armitage moves the meeting on to any other business.

I gather my bag, jacket and scarf and leave the meeting before he finishes. I follow one corridor then another, and go downstairs, finally emerging into the car park, which is not where I came in. I glance round for a moment, disorientated.

Everything changes, I think.

The cold has intensified and there is actually a mist. It is almost an autumnal evening. I can hear my footsteps tapping across the car park.

It is the nature of things to change, I tell myself.

Then I'm crying with unexpected force, sobbing and gasping in the middle of the council car park.

It's all lost, I think.

Starting suddenly, my tears suddenly stop. I pat my face lightly and quickly all over with a tissue like my mother used to do, then continue walking decisively towards the road. On the edge of the car park I stop and consider the way.

It is a spectral light. All sounds are muffled and the texture of air on my skin is different, softer. Blurred lights blow cones of radiance along the street.

I make out the bus stop in the distance and walk towards it, expelling long smoky breaths. It is unreasonably cold, I think. It isn't autumn yet.

I stand by the bus stop on the empty street. No cars pass. Perhaps they have given up the unequal battle with the roadworks. I look along the length of the street. Roadworks, scaffolding, boarded-up windows. I have a vision of the human race working like insects on the past, digging up what is already there, making it new. We turn over our human past, and feed off it, and change its form.

Slowly I become aware of another figure approaching through the mist, with a strange, loping step.

Why didn't I bring the car? I think, with a burst of passion.

– All right? says Nigel Scowcroft.

– Fine, thank you, I mutter.

– I was a bit worried about you, he says, being on your own, like.

– I'm fine.

– You have to be careful, you know.

Just don't say anything, I tell myself. I don't have to talk.

– Anyway, I've brought you some petition forms, he says, holding them out.

– What for?

He looks surprised.

– I was under the impression, I say, that things have been decided.

– Oh, you can't give up now, he says. – Fun's only just started.

I look at him for several moments without speaking.

– I'm not taking any more petition forms, I say.

– Oh, he says.

I return to staring along the road.

– It's a pity about this fog, he says. – I was hoping to see the Pleiades tonight.

I say nothing.

– Course they do say, he goes on, that there'll come a time when we can't see the stars at all, for light pollution. Imagine that. Looking up and just seeing like an orange glow. No stars.

Go away, I think.

– Well, if you think what the sky must have been, a hundred or even fifty years ago – blazing with stars. The war – that'd've been a good time. I mean, whatever else people went through, they could stand in a field and see from one end of the universe to another.

Now we can send spaceships out to them, but we can't stand in a field and look at them.

It's true, I think. But it's still Nigel Scowcroft I'm stuck here listening to, without a bus in sight. And it occurs to me again that he must have some peculiar effect on buses.

– Of course, most of the universe is invisible anyway, he says. – Ninety per cent of it, in fact. Dark matter.

I glance involuntarily at the sky.

– Oh, not dark like the sky, he says at once, dark in the sense you can't see it, but it's there around you all the time.

He moves his hands through the space between us as though through something that no one can see. I step back quickly, and he steps forward.

– They say that though you can't see it, feel it or touch it, it's the most powerful force there is, he says, in hushed tones, and behind him in two long rows the street-lamps crane their necks towards him like aliens.

– It shapes the galaxies and guides them, he says, pulling them along. It's a strange thought, isn't it? That something we know nothing about is shaping the universe, making us what we are –

– You mean like God? I snap.

Unexpectedly Nigel snickers.

– Who knows, who knows? he cackles.

I look at him with absolute dislike.

– You mean you do?

Again Nigel seems pleased, if anything, that I am responding to him at all. He is close enough for our breath to mingle, and I have the sudden sense of being very alone with him on the dark street.

– All I'm saying, he says, is that it's what we can't see that counts.

I stare at him. In my mind's eye an endless stream of lost people march between us: all the workhouse people, my mother, Martha, Millicent, Jamal.

Nigel nods, very seriously.

– The bus, he says.

It is the bus, gliding towards us silently through the mist.

CHAPTER 22

After much prevarication (he's rung me, twice now/I don't want to encourage him/I can't just leave without saying goodbye) I ring Dan.

    – Dan, it's Louise.

    – Who?

A good start, I think.

    – Louise.

    – Oh.

    – I was wondering whether the picnic might still be on?

    – Picnic?

    – The weather's brightened up.

    – Hm.

    – And I might be leaving soon.

    – Hmm?

    – Well – we said we would.

    – I suppose we could.

    – Try not to get carried away.

    – No, sorry, it's fine.

    – It's just that I've got the letters.

    – Letters?

    – The ones Eveline told us about.

    – Oh, I see.

    – Well, we don't *have* to –

    – No, no – I'd love to.

Pause.

– Well, when are you free? I say brightly. – Tomorrow? If it's fine?

– Tomorrow afternoon. I'll pick you up. OK?

Well, that was hard work, I think crossly, putting my phone away. I consider the possibility that Mary was entirely wrong about Dan, he isn't interested at all. I return to poring over the gaps in my family tree, already regretting the picnic.

Maybe it'll rain, I think.

The next day the sun is shining in a pristine sky. Dan picks me up with a show of good humour, but there is something else behind his eyes.

He didn't really want to come, I think.

We drive as far as we can up Harrop Ridge, then walk. The sky is a vivid, unchanging blue beyond light-coloured hills. When the wind blows, the grass is set in motion like a blond sea.

When we are out of breath we sit down not far from a fast-running stream. Surprised sheep scarper at our approach. I have brought the elderflower wine, which has begun to fizz in a promising kind of way, and a cake made without sugar or fat. Dan has brought chicken salad, from Sainsbury's, I think. The wine is surprisingly good, but Dan's face changes when he tries the cake.

– Hm. Nice texture.

I laugh at him.

– It'll grow on you, I say.

I sit on an outcrop of grass and tell him about Mary Brennan.

– So – you've got the letters.

– That's right.

– Well – what do they say?

I look at him.

– That bad?

– She seems to have killed her husband, I say, watching him carefully without appearing to, but no one knows what happened to her.

Dan whistles.

– There was a fire, you see, I say. – She shut him in, as far as I can gather – or, at least, didn't help him to get out.

Dan isn't sure what to say, I can tell. He's not sure why I'm so bothered.

– Family skeletons, eh? he says. – Well, I can see why they kept that one quiet. Have you got the letters with you?

I hand him the envelope. It's his family too. Then I sit, hugging my knees on the tufted grass and looking out towards Blackshaw Edge. Beyond it, just out of sight, is the workhouse, invisibly present. I tell him about the background to the letters, and Charles's birth.

Dan takes out large, rather old-fashioned glasses and, after a moment's awkwardness, puts them on. I watch him reading the spidery slant that is Millicent's handwriting, the larger coils of Anne's.

If I had a last wish it would be to see her, Millicent wrote.

– It certainly seems incriminating, Dan says at one point.

I say nothing. I'm suddenly seeing them all in the context of this landscape, of the land divisions and battles and enclosures, of the Elizabethan Poor Law, 1601, above all of the land itself, marking out the contours of their lives.

– Well, says Dan, it's certainly an amazing story.

– The secrets people keep, he says, and I wonder suddenly if he's thinking of Sandra. I am thinking about Jamal, and the way we came together from our separate histories, our different cultures. And yet we understood each other, or we thought we did. I thought we understood one another's pain.

There is a long silence. On the blond hillside a single tree stands perpendicular to the slope, like a man about to throw himself off.

Dan says, Didn't you say you were married once?

It's his barrister technique, I realize, to put out a question suddenly, like a snake puts out its tongue. This time I'm not shocked.

– I didn't, I say, but yes, I was.

I married Martin, a boy I knew at school. Not immediately after: three or four boyfriends had elapsed when Martin returned, an almost completely trained accountant, working already for a firm. We went out together for two years in the regular way. His brother was an estate agent, so when it came to marriage we got a nice house. Both sets of parents were very pleased.

My name was Pearson then.

I wouldn't have children, and Martin wanted two, a boy and a girl. I wasn't so enthused about replicating our genes, or about fitting any more neatly into the pattern laid out for me. After eleven years or so I applied for a job in London, got it and moved out.

My mother never forgave me.

– A nice man like Martin, she said, often. – A good husband. A good job. You must be soft in the head.

This was after we had established that Martin neither beat me nor slept around; that, moreover, I hadn't left him for anyone else, which she would have disapproved of, absolutely, but could have understood.

Visiting my mother made me very unhappy at that time, but it wasn't anything I could give up. Leaving Martin made me unhappy too, because of the amount of approval I lost. I didn't automatically feel strong and free. More like a newly hatched chicken tottering around with its head still stuck inside its shell.

One day, years later, my mother said everything she'd been carrying around inside her. She'd never known what had possessed me; marriage was no picnic, God knows hers certainly hadn't been, but she'd learned to live with it. She was no Catholic, but she couldn't see the point of divorce, swapping one state of affairs for another – And don't tell me, she said, drawing up her tiny, stocky frame and sticking out her considerable chin, that you just got bored. Boredom's a wicked word. It's a sin and a crime.

I started off listening, prepared for the worst. Grief (Martin as the son she'd never had), envy (I got out, she didn't), and censure in equal proportions, but by the end of the tirade I was covering my ears. Her words were like little hammer blows all over my skull.

– For God's sake, Mother, I said in the end, for God's sake – I don't know – all right? I wish I did. All I know is, I said, striving for accuracy, if I put coffee mats down he would go round after me, altering the angle of them all just a bit.

That stopped her. Briefly. I could see a penny dropping somewhere. But she pulled the shutters down quick as a wink, and went on instead about the money I'd thrown away, the house, no proper divorce settlement, I couldn't even do that properly.

– Coffee mats, she said.

And though I'd stopped listening I could see it all through her eyes, the lovely, successful marriage it was meant to be, and I thought suddenly, The future changes the past. Because when we married we were everyone's idea of the perfect couple, but now it would always be a mistake.

I give Dan the briefest outline of all this without looking at him. Only when I finish and he says, So you still don't know what made you leave? do I turn and look at him and say, No.

That was the frightening part, of course, that was the bald, frightening truth. Something I still don't understand caused all that wreckage, the loss of everything I thought I wanted.

And then Jamal.

I look back at the hillside, expecting some comment from Dan, some pronouncement.

It doesn't matter, I think.

It doesn't matter to my mother, her ashes scattered with my father's over her favourite flowers. It doesn't matter even to Martin, though for a time after I left I cherished fears for his safety and sanity. In fact, he married again, is now partner in the firm he worked for, and his wife is pregnant with their second child.

I should leave people more often.

The only thing that matters, I can see now, gazing at the teetering tree, is the force that made me leave, that jammed my foot down on that accelerator.

That violent, inexplicable force.

Dan doesn't say anything. When he does speak his voice is more hesitant than I have yet heard it.

– I – wasn't quite straight with you the other day.

Oh, no, I think. Revelation.

I told you Sandra took the kids away. That's not quite true. I'd never have let her do that. She left at Easter and I haven't seen her since. But she kept writing to Melanie and Mark. And the letters came after I'd left for work or I'd have binned them. As it was, Melanie kept them all. And the night after her exams she came to me – it was late, I remember – I was up late, drinking, I did a lot of that. She showed me the letters – all of them begging the kids to go over. Then she said, I want to go.

He pauses. Takes a swig of the elderflower.

– I came up with every argument I could think of – nothing budged her. In the end I had nothing left to say. The next thing I know I'm buying tickets and taking them to the airport. I remember standing there while they boarded. I felt like cutting my throat. And I must have looked as bad as I felt, because Melanie turned back. – We'll be back, Dad, she said. And that was it. I've heard nothing since then. Until yesterday – I had a note from Sandra saying the kids want to stay on a bit longer, and would I sort things out with the school. Nothing from them, no card, nothing.

There is a heavy silence. I remember his preoccupied manner on the phone, how I thought it reflected on me.

– I didn't tell anyone, Dan says, because, well, I just felt stupid. I've signed my own death warrant, haven't I, just handing them over? Now all I can do is wait. Not something I'm used to doing, that – nothing.

– You could go over, I say.

Dan has thought of this. He will go over if it comes to it. But if they don't want to come back with him, what then? Kidnap them? Involve the police?

– Perhaps you could write to them, I say, but he has already written.

– If it's what they want, he says. – I could fight Sandra, but I'm not fighting them. I just want to know it's what they want.

I reach over and press his arm. There are no choices, I think.

– They will come back, I say. I lean towards him and kiss his cheek. Then we look at one another and I can see the different shades of blue in his iris, the small contractions of his pupil.

Of course we make love. And it isn't at all bad. It makes me forget about the bumpiness of the ground, about Martin, my mother, Jamal; even, momentarily, myself. At one point I open my eyes but I'm not seeing him. What I'm feeling is a quickening in my flesh, a movement in the cells of my flesh towards life.

I even forget about Martha, though almost my first thought afterwards, as I ease myself up is, I bet she never did that. Bonked someone she didn't know too well on a bare hillside. Though, really, who knows?

Dan gets up and trots towards the stream.

– What are you doing? I say.

– I haven't done this for years, he says, peeling off socks and stepping tenderly into the water.

– Ow – ow – it's cold.

I laugh at him. Pudgy schoolboy paddling.

– Of course it's cold.

He carries on paddling and splashing, like a great, ungainly penguin.

– We used to look for gold up here, he says. – Aren't you coming in?

– I don't think so.

– Come on.

– No, thanks.

He steps out and runs towards me and I run away from him up the slope. Then he stops and picks something up, taking it back to the river.

– What are you doing? I say, hurrying back down. – What have you got there?

– We used to do this as well, he says, floating a paper boat. It is one of the letters.

– Dan!

– What? He is folding another one.

– You can't do that.

– Why not?

– Stop it, I say, but I'm starting to laugh. I kick off my sandals and go in after him. He splashes away.

– Give them back, they aren't mine, I say.

The third paper boat floats downstream. I catch up with Dan and try to snatch the remaining letters, but he holds them in the air, hugging me with his other arm.

– Come on, he says. – You have a go.

We are both laughing now. I take one of the letters and fold it the way he shows me, and off it goes on its uneven, bobbing ride. We make more and more and race them, a small fleet bobbing and floating beneath the intense, childhood blue of the sky.

CHAPTER 23

Martha

Cold days, eccles hanging, I light fire in Matron's room while scullery maid looks on. Matron has a mirror with three sides, and a lamp with a candle. When I move it about in front of the mirror I can see light curving on all sides, bending back on itself, over and over.

That's like time, I think.

Then big'un waps over, spite of her gammy leg.

– Tent door, she says to maid, and dings me so hard I cruckle to floor.

They know why I'm here.

– Play with fire, play by rules, says she, and gives me a reight lacing.

Then I'm ill.

Shamming. She'd be wur if she ailed owt.

Then everyone's ill. Wackert as foals and skellied. Skrikin on. Sick room's moaed eaut, and Matron's grandgin her teeth and roangin abeaut in a swat.

– Aw've had a chockful o' this, says big'un and leaves.

– Good shuttance, says I.

I keep sollit. In my mind I'm on the moor. I can hear moorpeeps and smell the sun.

The sun is a star, burning and turning, with all the millions of stars that come and go.

The stars are dust that's been here since the universe began. Like the dust of my body, that was the dust of stars and will be again, burning and turning for ever and ever amen.

Stars inside and stars out. Some people stand so as you can't see either, for the shadow they cast.

Them people have to go.

There shall be no darkness nor dazzling but one equal light.

Tears in my eyes are water that the dinosaurs drank.

Atoms of dinosaurs in your body, telling you what to do.

I don't tell this to the doctors or the nurses or any of the people.

They think I don't know where I am, but I know.

Aw'm in Queer Street wur thur's no back dur.

I grow thin as cat pepper, and one person bends over me then another.

I never speak to them.

I say nowt.

Sssh.

CHAPTER 24

Louise

Here is another photograph: me and my mother by her garden gate. She is shading her eyes against the sun, which makes her look as though she's smiling. I look as though I have my arm around her.

They say the camera never lies.

Of course, if I had put my arm around her she would almost certainly have shrugged it off. And if Jamal took it, as I think he did, the first time we all met when she was still being stiffly polite, she wouldn't have been smiling.

Even so, when I found it in her bedroom, among so much other stuff, I slipped it into my handbag. I think it was because, for that one time, we actually looked like mother and daughter.

Which is why I hesitate now, to put it in the album.

Then I think, Well, why not? As if the truth was ever something that could be reproduced, as if all these other photographs somehow stand for it.

So I put it in anyway, moving some of the other photographs closer together, and remembering vividly as I do so the sound of my mother singing to the radio, not only out of tune, but an entirely different tune from the one playing. If 'Only The Lonely' came on my mother would start singing 'Lead Kindly Light', or 'When I Fall In Love'. It was as if the music sparked off some older memory, or as if her relationship to the reality around her was always more tangential than it appeared, than her life had allowed it to be.

I smooth the plastic down round the edges of the photograph. That was my mother, I think.

It has taken me a long time to get this far, back to where I started from.

When my mother was alive I could hold on to the perceptions I had of her, the meanness and prejudices, the pain she caused. Death makes a different picture.

Then I turn to the family tree, filling it in as far as I am able, gaps and all.

There are still the things I will never know, about Martha, or Cora and Victor, about my mother. But it doesn't matter any more. It's as if I can see all my actions since leaving her rolling past me on a great screen: Martin and the marriage my mother never had, Jamal and the relationship she never would have had, my career, my search for Martha, all part of the running away that was really, all the time, bringing me back. Back to this landscape, my mother, and the family line.

Finally I write up my notes. And find myself telling it all like a story, my story, as if the different sections fit together after all.

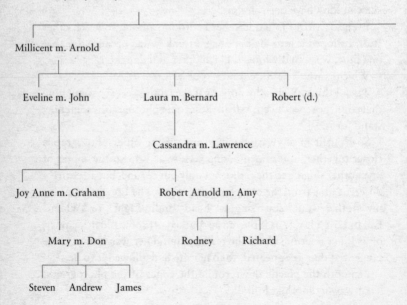

Well, what Paul wanted was a story.

I sit at the little table in the kitchen. I have managed, finally, to half open the window. Papers flap and dust flies up. Dust in the air that might have been there when the Romans came to Broadstones. Or when Martha was here. That might be Martha, I suppose. My mistake lay in trying to put it together, into a reconstituted person.

I write a little, pause, write a little, pause. I am watching the elder, which is heavy with berries now, tap and brush against the window. I can tell this story many different ways. The people in it change, according to the way I tell it. This is the way I'm choosing to tell it now.

Louise's Story

A long time ago, in 1870, a young girl called Emma Whately arrived at the workhouse above Broadstone Moss. Possibly she travelled in one of the wooden vans used to transport the destitute. I imagine her looking out from the back of it at

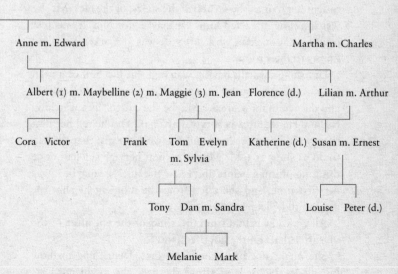

the receding villages as the van jolted and rocked over every stone. There would have been other people in the van with her: an old couple maybe, or a family with small children. Her own family, even, though there is no mention of them.

We don't know her story, or the circumstances that led to this particular journey, on this sunny/wintry/misty day. In my imagination she is thin and ordinary-looking, but with pretty hair. She is thirteen or fourteen years old.

Once in the workhouse she would have to work, of course. Cleaning and scrubbing, washing and mending, feeding the animals, keeping the small children in order. She would sleep on a wooden plank in a room crammed with other women balancing on their planks; their breathing loud and foul through the nights. There was only cold water to wash with, and workhouse clothes to dress in, yet somehow, in the course of her ordinary working day, she attracted the attention of Bernard Slater, Master of the Workhouse. Perhaps the light caught her hair as she scrubbed the stairs, or the fact that she was kneeling attracted him. Or maybe, for him, it was just routine. But one day, while his wife was at market, he called Emma to their room.

Did she go warily, having watched this big bull of a man around the other girls? Or eagerly, curious about his rooms and desperate for a break? Maybe she caught him watching her and smiled; it was survival after all. Did he tell her that there would be more food and less work, or just that she had to do as she was told? Maybe even at her age she had done this kind of thing before and knew the rules, or maybe it was her first time, and she cried from the moment he shut the door until he let her out.

All we know is that from this time, or the one after, or the one after that, Emma got pregnant.

She might not have known at first. Depending on how knowledgeable or how afraid she was, she might not have known until the third or fourth month. But we do know, or at least Alice Boardman told Irma Stowe, that she didn't keep it quiet. Reckless or unhinged, she did what no one else had done before, spoke openly about her condition, demanded a reduced workload, and frightened Bernard Slater.

Did he threaten her when he realized what was happening? He might easily have beaten her. But he seems to have felt power shifting in the mysterious way that power can. There was his wife, after all, his job, his reputation. Men and women were separated at the workhouse door precisely to stop the internal population growing. And then there was Alice Boardman, saying her fateful words to Henry Hawkyard. Plenty will, she said, when I tell them.

Alice was sacked, of course, and went back to her mother and son in Castleton, to face the years of starvation that killed first one then the other. And Bernard Slater came up with a solution involving herbs and an apothecary, at least the second apothecary he tried.

Did he convince Emma that an abortion would be the best thing all round? That it would be fine, even at this late stage in her pregnancy? Or that what he was giving her was medicine, to soothe the troubles of pregnancy and labour?

I don't suppose he meant to kill her. But in her seventh month Emma went into labour. And when it became clear that she was dying someone sent for the vicar, and either Emma or Sarah Brigg, also pregnant and panicking, told him what had happened. The vicar took the baby away, either he or Emma named him Charles, and went with Sarah to the Board of Guardians.

That was the end of Emma Whately, heroine, anti-heroine, workhouse girl, mother. She would have been buried in the paupers' part of the church graveyard, where what remains of her is buried still. She was just fourteen or fifteen years old.

A brief, unclean struggle ensued. Bernard Slater made false accusations against both Emma and Sarah, then the first apothecary he had visited stepped forward and he lost his job. Nothing was proved, they said, but soon after Henry Hawkyard retired. The vicar took the baby, but at some point he was delivered back to the workhouse, where there was a new Master and a new Clerk.

What happened to Bernard Slater? No one seems to know. We all know what happened to Hawkyard, but that's jumping the story.

Charles grew up. This is another gap that a story might fill. We don't know what it was like to be a workhouse child, to learn to crawl and speak and think within those walls. Who was kind to him? Who changed him when he wet the bed, or looked after him when he was sick? Who played with him?

Against all expectations, he survived.

One person who watched him grow up was Henry Hawkyard, now owner of the Old Hall, another was Alice Boardman. Alice had returned to Broadstones, begging by the market, and by one of those twists of fate that change history, met Nellie Flitch, Hawkyard's cook. Nellie Flitch took her on as scullery maid, and Hawkyard, out of charity or malice, allowed it. We know that she sometimes cleaned at the workhouse when no other cleaners could be found. Did she take a special interest in Emma's boy, since her own son had died? Or was she even then harbouring thoughts of revenge, and fostering them in him?

Charles was apprenticed to Enoch Wrigley, a Manchester bookseller. Superficially, at least, he was one of the lucky ones, given that many apprentices died and others were beaten witless, and of no further use from their teens. Others, thousands of others, were taken from their parents and shipped away, to Canada or Australia . . .

. . . I stop writing for a while as this vast, anonymous stream of children passes in my mind. Expendable as children always are, perishable tools of trade. I can see their eyes, searching the crowds for parents, I see the rhythmical flicker of legs and feet as they board . . .

There were men involved in organizing this, a network, Mrs Stowe said, though I can't imagine who they were at all. A business organization with occult overtones, maybe, a more sinister version of the Masons, promoting the interests of their members, interesting themselves especially in children, in the placing of apprentices. If they existed today they might be arranging for the organs of poor children to be transplanted into the bodies of the elderly rich, or catering for the special sexual preferences of clients. I find it impossible to imagine people like this, their faces, the language they use. Only the children are real to me, their pale feet drumming by.

This is my inheritance, I think.

A breeze blows, my paper lifts and falls, I return to my story.

It seems that Henry Hawkyard was involved with the placing of apprentices. He may have known Enoch Wrigley, or Enoch may also have been a member. I am unclear about this. But I think that Charles grew up knowing the story of his birth. I think Alice Boardman told him some time before he left the workhouse in 1882. I think that he returned to the Old Hall when he was nineteen or twenty years old, inflamed with a young man's passion for revenge, and that Alice Boardman let him in.

I do not know any of this, but it fits with my story.

I can see him plainly, wrapped in his muffler, carrying a pistol and a knife, following the corridor to the dining room where Henry Hawkyard sat, waiting for his food. Beneath his muffler his face is an agony of terror and rage. He is terrified that he will do this thing, he is more terrified that he will not. He deserves it, he tells himself over and over again, it's what he deserves. The door swings open, Henry Hawkyard looks up . . .

Did he murder Bernard Slater as well? I don't know. All I

know is that some years later, an alliance was arranged between Charles, named Wrigley after his guardian, and Martha Hopkins, my great-great-aunt. It was common for servants to have their marriages arranged, why not apprentices? It was better for a young man running a business if he was married. Maybe Enoch knew Martha's father, and maybe Martha's father needed help. At any rate it was arranged, I think, so that Charles would be in a better position to inherit the business, and then obligingly Enoch died.

I will never know the story of Martha's marriage, apart from the ending. There was a fire, and Charles was in the attic when it started, but then the door was locked from the outside and Martha disappeared. Did she start the fire, or just lock the door? Either way, what drove her to that point? And what happened to her afterwards?

In my mind I can see her turning the key in the lock, then closing the door on the smoking house, pressing the flat of her back against the outside door. It was night time, clear and cold. Was her mind full of jumbled voices or clear for the first time, clear as a star in the sky? She had no time to pick up even a few basic possessions. She walked to the end of the street and turned the corner. Out of sight, out of history, out of the family line . . .

These are the gaps I can't fill in. I'm giving you the story so that you can fill them in yourself. If you can use any of this material for your Project please feel free . . .

I stop writing. From the gaps in my story one person then another steps forward: Emma, Alice, Bernard, Henry, Charles and Martha. According to how I tell it, each person is either victim or oppressor, even Bernard, even Henry. I am aware of choosing my victims.

But somewhere in the process of writing I have also become aware that both these faces are mine. I have felt like a victim, but I have had my victims, my mother, Martin, Jamal. And in this way, finally, the faces of those unseen men who controlled the lives of children become real to me; they have human faces, after all.

The window stirs and creaks, and a leaf blows in, disturbing the dust again. I have written out my story as fully as I can, in order to let the dust that is Martha settle. Now that I've finished, I slip the papers into a file I bought specially for this purpose, and prepare to take it to Paul.

I slip my jacket on, reflecting that if I stayed here any longer I would need warmer clothes, then pause a moment considering the things I have to do. I want to take copies of the story and the family tree for Mary Brennan, in exchange for the lost letters, and for Dan, whose family line may still increase, while I am at the end of mine. Melanie and Mark can add to it, or Mary Brennan's sons if they're interested. Then there's Frank. I might see Frank later at the pub where I have arranged to see Dan for a final drink, but it might be nice if I called in on him myself. Finally, I have to choose a present for Mary.

My time here is over. I can't say why this is, but I know it to be true.

Last night I had the dream again. Jamal waiting for me in the colourless room. He was sitting on a bench, his face half turned away, half light half shade, the way I remember him. I feel all the old feelings, horror and shame. My mouth moves but no words form. Slowly I make my way over to the bench. I pause a moment then sit beside him. He doesn't look at me or speak. I sit with him and he with me, and we remain that way a long time.

Checking finally that I have all the papers I need, I leave by the back way, through the garden, determined to see if I can find my way to town by an old route I used to know, thus avoiding the clogged roads.

It has rained all night, and there are great round leaves containing water, and quivering flowerheads. The cow parsley has turned to brown stalks, but rosehips are reddening by the gate. The spider webs are brilliant with water as I brush past, tiny drops running into bigger ones that become very round and full.

Then I'm on the track I've never followed before, and there is an enormous puddle, and the darting flight of a wagtail across it, and in the field lapwings pecking the ground rise suddenly and silently, flashing black white black white black. Patches of brilliant light flare between clouds, a black wing shines green, a single bird tumbles into many and all the leaves on the trees lift and flicker in the wind and sun. Lines become curves and one thing changes continually into another in the colour and brilliance and movement of the world.

And soon the track broadens to a path, and the path becomes a small street, and in no time at all I'm in the back streets behind the library.

Paul is the first person I see, behind the main desk, stamping books repetitively and handing them back. I wait awhile, watching him. It is the aura of seriousness and care that attracts me, that attentiveness to the moment in hand.

When he sees me finally he finishes handing over a set of books then smiles suddenly, as if he has considered carefully before permitting himself to smile.

I approach the desk.

– There you are, I say, putting the file down in front of him.

– What?

– Stories, I say, about the workhouse. – And my family tree.

– Oh, *right*, he says, opening the file. He seems vague.

– I left you a message, I say. – Didn't you get it?

– No, I did – thanks very much.

– I thought you might be able to use the stories, I say, if your pageant idea comes off.

– Thank you very much, he says again. Then he looks at me closely and to my annoyance I'm suddenly shy.

– You don't think it's a bad idea, then, he says.

– I don't, I say, it's not. I shake my head vigorously to underline this.

He leafs through one page after another.

– You've done a lot of research, he says, then, How did you find out all this? and I tell him, filling in the details as he reads.

– This is great, he says, and I feel a pang of embarrassed joy. I stare at the brown curve of his parting, the mole on the side of his neck.

Not for me, I think.

Carol glances at us sharply, then takes over the queue. Paul turns the pages more slowly now, considering.

– How's the fund-raising going? I ask.

He pulls a face.

– You mean it might not happen?

– Oh, it'll happen, he says, looking up at me, his eyes very clear. – I'm going to a meeting later today, in fact.

Another meeting, I think.

– Well, it's a start, I say.

The door opens and there is a blast of air. I had forgotten that the schools have gone back, but here they are, tiny children in uniform pouring by. There is a rhythmical flicker of white socks, grey socks, trainers, boots.

Paul watches too, momentarily mesmerized, then he turns back to me.

– Maybe we could go out for a drink sometime, he says.

Well! I think. But I shake my head.

– I'm leaving, I say. – That's why I brought this in today.

I can't believe I just said that.

– Oh, Paul says, well, and for a moment I'm convinced he's going to say something else, something personal, then he reaches across the desk quickly and presses my hand.

– I'll have to go, he says, indicating the children's section, where the noise is escalating. He turns and waves my file at me before disappearing.

– Thanks a lot, he says, this is great. Really.

I remember to take the photocopies, smiling to myself all the time, and then leave the building, my heart foolishly lifted. The sky is sullen now, but the trees glow, and then the first shop I go into has the ideal gift for Mary-next-door: a teapot with a picture of an old lady watering flowers round the base.

So that is everything, all I have to do. I carry the teapot in a plastic bag along the street, still feeling the pressure of Paul's hand on mine, like a painless sting.

I'll never grow old, I think.

I have the notion that I want to say goodbye to the places I've come to know and so take a slightly complicated route back, one turning after another, becoming slightly disorientated. At the end of every street the great hills rise blue with heather, though I can see history written on them in stone-wall enclosures that have divided them into smaller and smaller squares, the housing estates creeping further and further up the sides, each shifted boundary marking another battle lost by the Residents' Association. This landscape will never be the same for me, I think. And neither will London, because if this place has changed for me then London must.

I follow the line of the nearest hill, beginning to feel tired. I'm not far from Frank's, though, and I intend to call in with the photocopies and say goodbye. But when I get to Frank's, with the black mass of broom near the gate, I realize that all the curtains are closed.

June, I think, chilled, and after hesitating a moment I turn away. I don't want to disturb anyone. And I tell myself that Frank might be in the pub later on, though this is unlikely if anything has happened to June.

I go on my way more soberly now, passing through the little ginnel at the side of their house. Me and Dan won't happen, I reflect, any more than me and Paul will, though it might have been nice, was nice. But we have our different tracks to follow. Besides, he wants his wife back.

And as I approach the little playground I'm feeling quite low. Everything's over, I think.

I walk towards the playground, which is empty now, as it was the last time I saw it from Mrs Stowe's window. I locate her window and wonder if she is still watching from it, unchanged. It occurs to me that it is a terrible thing not to change.

Then as I draw near the playground I see that there is a child after all, a little boy, standing quite still by the swings. As I approach he throws himself on to the nearest swing, stomach first, running forward then lifting his feet to swing back.

– Hello, I say, but he doesn't respond, the way that children don't, always. He is an ordinary-looking boy in worn clothes, with silky, colourless hair.

– What's your name? I say, and this time he does answer.

– Tom, he says, and I have the sudden sensation that we are very alone. Just us and the blind, blank windows of the terraced houses, the creak, creak, creak of the swing. I feel the need to speak, and think of saying, That's a nice name, in a stupid, grown-up kind of way, or Shouldn't you be at school?

Instead I say nothing, but glance upwards at the metal framework, which is old, flaking and rusting in patches, gravel rather than cushioning beneath the swings. I think of all the little boys who have ever played here.

– I can do this, Tom says, and he twists the swing round to the point of maximum tension then lets go, swinging round and round.

I suppress another grown-up urge to say, Don't do that, it's bad for the swing, and just watch him twist it round again.

– That's the best bit, isn't it? I say, as he stands poised, ready to fly off again. He looks at me silently then lets go, swinging round and round and from side to side.

I leave him there, looking back over my shoulder from time to time, half expecting him to disappear, but he's still there, spinning and swinging, oblivious to the landscape around him, all the conflicts and divisions. I glance back until he has receded almost to the point of disappearing, the point where he becomes invisible, like the invisible pressure of Paul's hand on mine, or the body of my mother; invisible and powerful, like the mystery of the world.

Glossary

afterings	the last milk from a cow
beestings	the first milk from a newly calved cow
bellin	bawling
bellweather	noisy woman
besom	stroppy woman
best bib and tucker	best clothes
bided	put up with
blobmeauth	loud-mouthed gossip
brawson	fat, lusty
cack-handed	clumsy
cauve	calf
clemmed	starving
clockin hen	said of a garrulous woman
cob	throw
cock on his own midden	well-to-do, rules his own roost
cocks his toes and slips off catch	dies
cranky side eaut	bad-tempered
croot	crooked
croping and crappling	creeping and crawling
cruckle	to sink down
dinged	upbraided, got at
donkey looks	mournful looks
eautcumblins	outsiders
eccles	icicles
first cock o' hay fears cuckoo away	get in first
flited	vexed
fly op wi' hens	act from feeling the pinch of poverty
fratch	upset yourself, take on

fussocks	fat, idle woman
goin deawn like watter in a dych	failing in health
gosterin iron	special iron for the collars of shirts
grandgin	grinding
hang yed like pown heaund	hang your head like a whipped dog
haver	kind of bread sauce
hopple	hobble
hutherin wind	loud, roaring wind
jiggered op rump and stump	bankrupt
kalling	idling, gossiping
kegley on her pins	unsteady on her feet
kibe	to draw the mouth crooked in contempt
killin hisself to keep hisself	overwork
lacing	beating
lant	urine
limb	limb of Satan
latching	infectious
meyl	meal
mithered	worried, harassed
mizzy	quagmire, confusion
moaed	crowded
moance, moangy	mess, messy, shiftless
moonpennies	daisies
moorpeeps	grouse
mowdiwarp	mole
mullock	dirty, slovenly person
mullycrushed	hopelessly ruined, beyond repair
nesh	tender, soft
nethercrop	spider
nobbut	nothing but
ovish	clownish
peauchin over slattered milk	crying over spilt milk
pulin	whining
queer as two cross sticks	difficult
roangin	shouting angrily

scrannil	a thin, underfed person
segs	patches of hard skin
shepster	starling
shuttance	riddance
skellied	shaky
sken	look at
skrikin	crying
sollit as a box	silent
sowd horse and bowt donkey	come down in the world
suddlin	twirling clothes in a tub
swat	passion, fit
swither	burn fiercely
twitcher	swindler
wackert	weak
waps	skips
wezilled	crinkly, withered
worrited	harassed
wur nur	worse than
yawnecked	twisted